FALL DOGS

FALL DOGS

A Novel

DAN ROSENBERG

SANTA FE

Sunstone books may be purchased for educational, business, or sales promotional use. For information please write: Special Markets Department, Sunstone Press, P.O. Box 2321, Santa Fe, New Mexico 87504-2321.
Cover design › Dan Rosenberg
Book design › Vicki Ahl
Body typeface › Cambria
Printed on acid-free paper

———————————————————————————

Library of Congress Cataloging-in-Publication Data

Rosenberg, Dan, 1943-
  Fall dogs : a novel / by Dan Rosenberg.
    pages cm
  ISBN 978-0-86534-932-2 (softcover : alk. paper)
  1. Young men--Fiction. 2. Alaska--Fiction. 3. Time travel--Fiction.
I. Title.
  PS3618.0831655F355 2013
  813'.6--dc23
                        2013001995

———————————————————————————

WWW.SUNSTONEPRESS.COM
SUNSTONE PRESS / POST OFFICE BOX 2321 / SANTA FE, NM 87504-2321 /USA
(505) 988-4418 / ORDERS ONLY (800) 243-5644 / FAX (505) 988-1025

DEDICATION

To southeast Alaska and its people; the
inspirations that allowed my imagination to take wing.
And special thanks to the Skinna family of Klawock, Alaska
who will always have a warm place in the hearts
of my wife Susan and me.

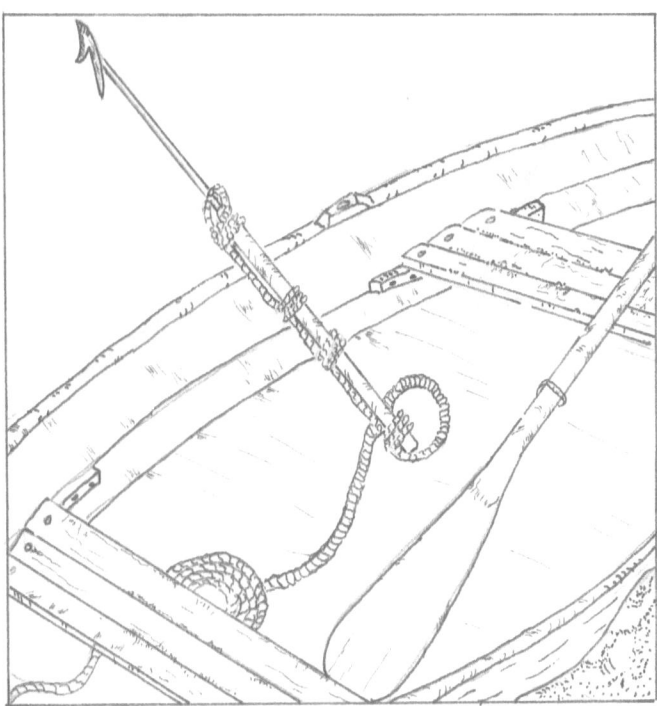

ALASKA

56°00'

Prince of Wales Island

55°30'

Noyes I.D.

Steamboat Bay

Klawock

Craig

Tlevak Narrows

Dall It

Tlevak Str.

Cordova Bay

Kaigani

Devils Reef

Pacific Ocean

54°32'

Ketchikan Saxman

Metlakatla

ACKNOWLEDGMENTS

To my wife Susan for her encouragement and support throughout the writing of this book.

Also to Patti Sedberry (Stonewall County Library), Martha Jones (Aspermont Economic Development Corporation), and Stephenia Mullen (Aspermont Chamber of Commerce) who on numerous occasions volunteered their help to make copies of my manuscript.

And also to my editor, James Clois Smith Jr. (Sunstone Press) who gave me the opportunity to publish this, my first, novel.

INTRODUCTION

It's all about the order of life. Winter is gone, and so with the arrival of spring are the seaweeds, followed by the bait fish, then the salmon, and finally comes the fishermen.

Southeast Alaska is an archipelago of a thousand and one islands. Its rugged mountain ranges rise straight up from the sea fifteen thousand feet or more; eternal mammoths with their patchwork cloaks of white and green, deep and pure; snow and glacier and virgin forests of weathered giants. Still standing are the Hemlock, Yellow and Red Cedar, and Spruce. They are the guardian brothers that have passed the test of time.

From the forest to the beach, like an alien sponge, is that deep peat like sphagnum cover, Muskeg. And the ocean here is cold and deep. This is truly a rugged land devoid of encumbrance where creatures run wild and the essentials are enough.

It is the sea that brings forth life, and on it all is dependent. Without the sea there would be no rain. And without the rain, this place would have no soul.

And the rains never fail.

1

THE NATURE OF THINGS

As spring changes to summer which becomes fall, then come the great schools of salmon. They come as if on cue. First the Pinks, followed by the Reds, the Kings, and finally the Chums. They all begin their lives in fresh water and then migrate to the sea. Following the coastline they first travel southward to the equator then on to circumnavigate the Pacific Ocean clockwise back to their natal stream. It is an amazing ability that is held deep within their DNA and passed from generation to generation as an essential and never failing instinct. It is more than a mystery and truly a wonder of nature after spending years at sea they are drawn home to that very pool where they began; now to reproduce and begin the cycle over again. The grand and disposable pompous male is always the first to arrive. By muscle and fang he stakes and defends his territory. It's his purpose.

But for the sake of diversity, the weak who by their cunning have survived, will also have a chance. It is the nature of things. That having been said, the female with her precious burden will then emerge from the depths to crowd the shallows. Here, she faces many dangers.

Predators in abundance are drawn to the spawning grounds and she is the entree. It is a numbers game and here amid the carnage she may survive to select the perfect place to build her nest where her offspring will be created. A dark safe place protected from the caprices of the surrounding world. How she does this may be explained as a mix of instinct and physical endurance. But again, one thing for certain, it is the nature of things.

By the hundreds of millions they begin as unblemished fragile pink spheres beneath the cobbles. Only the perfect place will do with its never ending upwelling current of pure fresh water, essential for life. Not too strong nor too weak. Not too warm nor too cold. Undisturbed in the dark they develop. Day by day and month by month fall becomes winter and winter becomes spring. And from that safe dark place the offspring will finally emerge after the great congregation has long since expired. Expired and adsorbed into the food chain to provide sustenance for the next generation of life that begins anew.

Whether from man-made or natural causes, their numbers are diminished. Emerging by the millions and millions, the minute fry hatchlings become the thousands and thousands of juveniles that will survive to enter the sea. Just a fraction of what squirmed out of the gravel will return as adults. It will work no other way. Again, it is the nature of things.

And it is the knowledge of this behavior that has been passed on from one generation of fishermen to the next. Trollers, gill netters, and seiners; these fishermen wait in a long line of predators. All with the common goal: to intercept matured salmon migrating south down the coast, back to where they began.

PART I
CHEECHAKO

2

NORTHERN ADVENTURE

Summer 1975 found me on the ferry Malaspina heading north from Seattle, Washington to southeast Alaska. The Malaspina, at four hundred and eight feet from stem to stern and a capacity for five hundred passengers, she is one of the largest and more comfortable of the fleet.

At the time, I was twenty two years old, fresh out of a four year enlistment in the U.S. Navy, and ready to embark on my Alaskan adventure before settling down to college and the rest of my life.

So with my backpack, sleeping bag, and three hundred dollars in my hip pocket, I joined the other cheechacos (newcomers) camping out on the back deck bound for America's last frontier.

We left port under a velvet cover of darkness on a three day voyage, through the "Inside Passage." It would carry us north along the coast of British Columbia, past Vancouver and the Queen Charlotte Islands; then across Dixon Entrance (forty miles of open water) into southeast Alaska and the Tongass Narrows to the dock at Ketchikan.

My shipmates were just as excited as I was. For one young couple, Peter and Helen Bronkowitz from New York, this was their honeymoon and they were determined to make the most of it. Having never been west of New Jersey, Peter said in his heavy Brooklyn accent, "yeah, everyone we know who got married went to Niager Falls, or Florider, or Atlantic City. So we decided," he put an arm around Helen whose face flushed pink at his touch, "to do something different."

Theirs will be a two week Alaska safari beginning at the Ketchikan waterfront where a little single engine chartered float plane waits for them, tied to the dock. For these two "city slickers," this will be a trip to remember.

Before boarding, all their gear will have to be packed into the rear of the plane. Once this is done, their next hurdle will involve stepping from the security of a relatively steady dock onto one of the plane's bobbing pontoons (one slip and it's into the ocean), then up a two or three rung ladder into the passenger cabin. Once they are buckled into their seats and after a short upwind full throttle taxi out onto Tongass Narrows, the plane will quickly ascend skyward to its cruising altitude (a few thousand feet). They will then make their way across one or more mountain ranges to the remote U.S. Forest Service lake front cabin they had reserved. One of many scattered throughout the seventeen million acre Tongass National Forest.

As standard routine, the pilot will circle the lake one time then land on the far end and taxi toward the cabin. Then timing it just right, he will shut the engine off and the plane will glide silently onto the beach. With pontoons grounded and without wasting time they will unload their baggage (he's anxious to get back to Ketchikan to pick up another fare as he's paid according to how many hours he spends in the air). After a minimum of chit chat, they will help him push the plane off the beach and nose it around into deeper water. The pilot will climb from the pontoon into the cockpit, shut the door and start the engine.

There they are, standing on the beach surrounded by all their belongings. The pilot will stick his head out the window and pass on a few parting words, "Watch out for bears." And, "See ya in two weeks."

The plane will idle farther out onto the lake and then after a moment or two the engine will accelerate. The noise most certainly deafening, Peter and Helen will turn with their backs to the prop wash. In a moment or two the plane, with its engine at full throttle, will taxi across the lake and vault (flaps up) back into the air. After circling the cabin one last time, their link to the outside world will disappear behind the surrounding mountain tops. Gone; and they are alone. Really alone!

Pete said, "Yeah this is gonna be a trip to remember." Then he handed me his camera and asked, "Hey, take our picture, will ya?" I obliged.

Their overstuffed backpacks were evidence of their resolve to guarantee that their adventure will be a success: insect spray, fishing rods and tackle, cameras, rain gear, survival rations, first aid kit, fire starter, extra clothing, etc. etc. I thought, "Where's the bear repellent?"

Then, there was an elderly couple from Detroit on their way to fulfill a pledge made years ago. George, the husband, told me, "I worked forty five years as a welder. Almost blind now, but me and my wife Edith," they smiled at each other, "have always talked about going to Alaska. Not sure why but something always got in the way. Now we're old, so it's now or never. We just had to make this trip."

I remember the six member Scottish bagpipe band on its way to the national bagpipe convention in Skagway. As they stood on the aft deck with the full moon at their backs and dressed in kilts, they played on and on well into the early morning hours. Their unique music resonated throughout the ship.

Some of us would search for summer jobs. For the most part the choices were limited to logging, tourism, or commercial fishing. And some like me were just going to see what was out there and take it one step at a time. We all had Alaska in common.

For me, just getting to the ferry was a challenge which began with my flight from Los Angeles International Airport (LAX) and an indicator light in the cockpit. After sitting on the runway for an hour or so, the plane was towed back to the terminal where everyone disembarked and waited for the problem to be fixed. Luckily for us it turned out only to be a burnt out bulb rather than a mechanical problem. Regardless, the scheduled two hour flight from Los Angeles to Seattle turned into six.

As luck would have it, my back pack was too large to fit into the overhead compartment and had to be checked in as baggage. I had previous experience with lost luggage and was rightly nervous about parting with my pack.

I remember that sweet little flight attendant telling me, "Relax sir, not to worry, very rarely are bags lost by our airline." She was so nice but such a liar.

So after landing in Seattle, I spent four more hours at the baggage terminal waiting for my backpack to be found. Then with no time to spare (time and tide wait for no man), I made my way via public transportation (taxis were on strike) to the ferry terminal. Late, but luck was on my side. It seems the ferry could not depart without a final inspection and the inspector was late. It turned out he was returning from his annual Hawaiian vacation and happened to be on the same flight as me (Karma was on my side). I actually had beaten him to the terminal. Boarding time was delayed two more hours.

By midnight, sleep caught up with me. I was so exhausted that the steel deck actually felt good. I closed my eyes and like a babe in his crib, was rocked asleep by the roll of the sea while the bagpipes played "The Hills of Loch Lohmond."

The next thing I knew, it was five o'clock the next morning and I was crawling out of my sleeping bag, eager to start the day. Scattered around me were swollen sleeping bags zippered shut. No movement. The air was cool, crisp, and invigorating.

Fully rested, I stood, faced the stern and stared at the prop wash that extended out behind us for what seemed miles and miles. It was deep water here. Sea gulls hovered above us, calling back and forth to each other. We were off the coast of British Columbia and to the northwest were the Queen Charlotte Islands. Dixon Entrance and Alaska were just beyond. An uncontrollable smile crossed my face. Like I had just taken the first step on the long road home it was a feeling of pure relief.

The smell of fresh brewed coffee wafted through the air from the cafeteria.

I sat at a corner table and ate my breakfast. Food tastes so much better aboard a ship. There were three of us in the dining room. The old man and his wife sat at another table holding hands and watching the scenery pass by their window. They were unaware of anyone else in the room. This voyage might be their last adventure together but that didn't matter. It was a new day. They made this trip together and were enjoying it as much as anyone else; or maybe more.

After breakfast, I made my way back outside and forward towards the bow. Not too many passengers up and about this early so I had the deck to myself. All was quiet. Save for the hiss of our wake against the hull, the sea was calm and glassy smooth. I just stood there lost in trance absorbing it all. Clear cold blue water, rocky shores, thick evergreen forests, and wildlife. Washed up on isolated beaches were the scattered remains of huge old tree trunks that offered proof of powerful past storms. Bald eagles soared and ravens called from the tree tops. Every now and then a migrating salmon on the last leg of its journey to a distant spawning ground would break the surface and jump two or three feet out of the water. Why they do this no one really knows. I've heard various opinions: they do it to shake hitchhiking parasites loose; the shock of their bodies slapping the water helps mature their eggs; to get a bearing on their location; or maybe they do it for the sheer enjoyment of it all. Whatever the reason, it's in their nature.

I was lost in daydream just leaning over the rail staring down at the water; totally mesmerized by the sight of a pod of dolphins surfing the wake at our bow. As I watched those superb beings glide through, under, and over the water, I felt a sense of privilege.

A deep but friendly voice from out of nowhere brought my daydreaming to an abrupt end. "Good morning."

Surprised, I answered, "Hi."

He said his name was Ben Selkirk and that he was a commercial fisherman returning home to Prince of Wales Island from a shopping trip in Seattle.

I smiled and said, "I'm Dylan Templeton." We shook hands. I asked, "Shopping trip?"

"Yes, fishing gear for our boat."

That answer sparked my interest. It turned out that he was a Tlingit (pronounced Kling-cut) of the Dog Salmon clan and his home was the village of Klawock (sounds like the call of the Raven) on the west coast of Prince of Wales Island. It is said, his people came to Alaska from somewhere else, possibly Polynesia, a time lost in the millennia, long long ago. He looked to be the same age as myself and obviously was a good fit for this rugged place. The look of someone used to a life of physical labor. Call it gut instinct or just a hunch, or whatever, I knew we would be friends.

He asked, "So what brings you to Alaska?"

I told him about my recent discharge from the navy and that as far back as I could remember, wanting to see Alaska, first hand. I finished by saying, "Well anyway this seemed like a perfect time to make the trip."

About that time it started to rain so Ben and I continued our conversation over coffee in the cafeteria. Ben's shopping trip to Seattle was the first time he'd been out of Alaska and I had the feeling he was a little homesick and just needed someone to talk to. He seemed as much interested in my life as I was in his. I told him about growing up in northern California. "We lived in Trinadad, not far from the Redwood forest. It was my mother, my two older brothers, and me. I never really knew my father; he was killed in a car crash when I was a baby. All of us worked in the vineyards and after graduating high school I enlisted in the navy so that I could get the GI Bill to pay for college after my enlistment was over."

"And what about you," I asked.

Ben said he never went past high school. It was more important for him and his village that he learn the skills of his father. As was true for all the men of his family, he became a fisherman. It was in his blood. His classroom was the deck of his father's boat and just like all deckhands Ben learned how to handle it all: the heavy lines, the net, the hydraulics, the rigging, the engine, the pumps, the electronics, and everything else that was a part of the boat.

And most importantly he learned how to be part of the crew. Someone they could depend on. And for Ben, his education began as soon as he learned to walk.

I admit I was a little envious of Ben.

I've done a fair amount of traveling, always looking for my place in the grand scheme of things and never quite finding it. Ben on the other hand, only rarely left Klawock but had found his. It may be when it comes to choices, less is better than more. In reality not everyone knows how to choose.

He asked, "Any plans?"

"No plans. Not sure what I'm gonna end up doing. I love to fish though. Never done any commercial fishing but I thought maybe I could get a summer job on a fishing boat just to give it a try."

Ben laughed. Over the years he'd met a lot of young men eager to "give fishing a try." Most who tried gave up before the end of their first season. Often they would brag how they could do this and that. Just to get hired. But it was just "talk," and when the work proved too much for them, they quit.

He looked at me a couple of times, sizing me up, smiled and said, "Dylan, I think you ought to go fishing with us."

I sighed, "Really?"

"Yep, we're gonna be leaving in a few days. One of our guys quit and we need a replacement. You'll like my dad and if he likes you, you're in," he paused, "he's a great skipper and you might make a lot of money, really!"

"Okay," I answered, hoping his father liked me. For the rest of the trip I listened to Ben talk about fishing in southeast Alaska while he listened to me about the navy and growing up in California.

As we passed the northeast tip of Graham Island, the most northern of Canada's Queen Charlottes, we left the protected calm of Hecate Strait and entered Dixon Entrance, an exposed forty mile stretch of open water.

Ben spoke from experience, "During the winter this can be a real bad place. Gale force winds over eighty knots and swells over sixty feet high and no place to hide. Lots of boats have disappeared around here." This was summer though and the sea was calm.

An hour or so later, and still in Dixon Entrance, we passed numerous small to medium sized islands (while many appeared to be less than a hundred yards end to end, others were more than five miles across).

Soon with Zayas Island on our port side and Dundas Island (both Canadian) on our starboard, we passed through the narrow Caamano Passage and shortly afterward into American water and Revillagigedo Channel.

The voice over the loudspeaker announced, "Ah, ladies and gentlemen," a brief pause, "for your information we will arrive at Ketchikan ferry terminal shortly." Soon after entering Tongass Narrows, Alaska's "first city" appeared on the north shore of the channel.

We remained inside the cabin and watched while our crew scurried about the deck and readied the Malaspina for docking. With just enough reverse gear, the ship came to a gentle stop in the calm water. Her starboard side was within twenty feet of the dock. What followed was a well-choreographed routine; flawless.

The crewman standing at the rail, cast (lasso style) a weighted line from the boat, down over the water, to his counterpart waiting on the dock below. One throw, that's all it took. That being done, that messenger line was then tied to the free end of the heavy hawser coiled on deck, fore to aft. Its opposite end wound a few turns, around the drum of the powerful bow winch. "Haul away," was the call from the ferry. The dock worker pulled the hawser through the forward chock and secured it dockside to a pair of over-sized bollards. Then the crewman on board turned from the rail and gave a "thumbs up" signal to the first mate at the bow who then engaged the clutch that set the winch in motion. With each slow turn of the drum a coil of manila line disappeared from the deck. Slack soon gone, the ship was pulled to the dock. A second hawser, in similar manner, was passed through the stern chock to the dock. The hawsers and steel hull plates groaned as the ship was pulled tight to the rubber bumpers bolted to the dock pilings. In just a few minutes the free roaming Malaspina was no more than an extension of the Ketchikan ferry dock.

The next sound from below was that of the steel car deck door sliding open along the ship's hull followed by that of the gangplank as it was pushed across the concrete dock and secured to the ferry.

The familiar voice over the loudspeaker announced, "Passengers are now free to move to the car deck and disembark. Have a nice day."

I said good bye to my shipmates and wished them good luck on their adventures.

We moved from the fluorescent light of the car deck and into a bright Ketchikan Monday morning. As we ascended the steep steel ramp from the dock to the terminal's parking lot I stared back through the rear window of Ben's Chevy, fixated on my back pack precariously balanced and teetering on top of an outboard motor; just waiting to fall from its perch off the back of the truck then roll either under the front wheels of the semi following us or into the ocean. Either way I was screwed.

"Don't worry," Ben said, "your gear's safe." Then, he pointed to the little ferry tied to the dock. "That's the Chilkat. It leaves tomorrow morning for Prince of Wales Island and we'll be on it. If the weather's good you're gonna enjoy the ride. We'll be here in Ketchikan today."

I thought, "What if the weather's not so good?"

Ketchikan, Alaska. Located on Revillagagido Island (the "locals" just call it Revilla Island), is like most coastal southeast Alaska towns: lots of rain; it's on an island; its back is against the base of a rugged mountain range; and its feet touch the Pacific. It's economy is export; mainly fish, minerals, and timber.

It was built in the late nineteenth-century by fishermen and miners. Shortly after the turn of the twentieth- century Ketchikan's population swelled to five thousand residents which made it the largest city in the state. Then as the mining industry stalled fishing took over and Ketchikan became the salmon canning capitol of the world; millions of cans.

It's a lot tamer now but at one time Ketchikan was a wild and "wooly" place. Back then there were a multitude of canneries, saloons, and whore houses. In this frontier town, law enforcement was at a minimum and violators of the law, depending on the severity of their crime, could either be thrown in jail or for the sake of expedience, bound to an appropriate piling at low tide to become crab bait with the incoming tide.

During the Prohibition Era, smuggling booze into the city, which sits little more than fifty miles from the Canadian border, was a relatively easy task. Not to be forgotten is The Red Light District of Ketchikan Creek which had the notorious reputation as the place "where men and fish came up the creek to spawn." It was a reputation that lasted until the 1950s. Although remnants of the past still exist, for the most part, Ketchikan is a "family town" now.

For over a hundred years, fishing was the primary economy of all coastal Alaska. Now, the great schools of salmon have all but disappeared as a result of a combination of mismanagement, greed, ingenuity, and ignorance. Some might say, "It's not a matter of good or bad but just cause and effect." I think they're wrong. Along with the decline of salmon in Alaska and due in large part to the above reasons, was the decline of forests throughout the Pacific Northwest (California, Oregon, and Washington).

All eyes turned on southeast Alaska's ancient Tongass National Forest. Dollar signs; trees meant money and jobs so the logging industry headed north to Alaska where timber became the mainstay, at least as long as the trees held out. They wouldn't. It became obvious that here as elsewhere, the industry had a catastrophic effect on the environment; another peg in the coffin. It's a delicate balance, healthy streams and healthy forests go hand in hand. Somehow though, as abusive as the logging industry was on the environment, just enough salmon have managed to survive to provide for Alaska's fishers. But of course that can change.

In just a few years the great stands of ancient trees within the Tongass disappeared and along with them, commercial logging. So the economy would shift again this time to tourism.

They come each year to experience the magic: tourists. Regardless of whatever happens, Ketchikan will always be a portal to the rest of Alaska. The town is a mix and match of modern and turn of the century architecture. All under the watchful eye of Deer Mountain who's four thousand foot peak is covered with snow throughout most years. Although mediocre by Alaskan standards, the mountain truly does have mystical qualities setting it apart from its bigger brothers too numerous to count.

Ketchikan is a blue collar town where the main employers are the log mills, the canneries and cold storages, the fishing fleet, tourism, and all that which support these industries.

It usually takes about twenty minutes to drive from one end of town to the other. On that day however, traffic was a bit slower. No matter, I was truly captivated by the rhythm of this little town which had come awake after a long winter's sleep. The harbors were filled with fishing boats and the docks were alive with fishermen. Some were working on their gear and others just meandered about burning up time waiting for the fishing season to begin.

While on shore a fisherman may or may not wear his rain gear (bib overalls and jacket), almost always he wears his red rubber boots.

Then there were the loggers. A proud bunch; their long sleeved cotton or wool work shirts were cut to elbow length and seriously frayed by the alteration. "Logger World" extra wide red suspenders support their tan canvas dungarees which like their shirts, are cut shin length and likewise, always frayed at the bottoms (a full length pant leg or sleeve are hazards just waiting to be snagged in the woods). A pair of caulked (hobnailed) leather boots tied together, shoestring to shoestring, hung over one shoulder. A chain saw in one hand, and a fully stuffed duffle bag in the other. And on their feet they wear red rubber boots. These lumbermen crowd the air taxi terminals waiting to be flown out on chartered flights to any one of a hundred and one remote logging camps where they will live and work until winter snows brings all activity to a halt.

Locals carrying on their normal day to day routines move back and forth along the sidewalks. It seemed like everyone wore red rubber boots except tourists who wear canvass or leather.

Clouds appeared and a light rain began to fall.

We passed under a banner, "Welcome Princess Patricia." Ben pointed to the channel. "Check it out!"

There moving along south Tongass Narrows was the little six thousand ton, red and white Canadian passenger liner, Princess Patricia. In high style, she was escorted down the channel by two fireboats whose water cannons directed a constant spray over the classic liner. While whistles blew and horns sounded; crowds stood along the waterfront cheering the ship's arrival. She was the beginning (a salvation of sorts) of a new era coming to Ketchikan and she meant as much to tourism here as the Spirit of St. Louis did to transoceanic aviation.

Ben stopped in front of the State Office Building. By the time I slid out of the truck's cab I had my instructions: buy your crewman's license at the commercial fisheries office; buy your rain gear and boots at Tongass Traders; and I'll meet you at the Sourdough at five pm. The last words I heard as the Chevy pulled away were, "and stay out of trouble." I felt a little uneasy as I stood there and watched the rear end of Ben's pickup truck and my pack disappear down the narrow street.

"Oh well," I thought, "whatever happens; happens. No need to worry now," and then, "Trouble, what kind of trouble?"

I entered the building.

The five men standing in front of the elevator were friends. I guessed fishermen. I asked, "You guys happen to know where they sell crewman licenses?"

They laughed. "Just follow us we're all going to the same place."

By the time we stepped out of the elevator we were kindred spirits on the road to become "crewmen" (hopefully).

The middle aged woman at the counter handed me my application which I filled out and handed back along with the one hundred dollar fee. She smiled, "It should be in the mail by the end of the week." Was it that obvious that I was just another young wannabe commercial fisherman? The next fellow in line, older than the rest of us (in his fifties, at least), moved forward with his application; he looked at her and said, "Yep, I'm gonna find me a skipper that needs a good crewman and make a lot of money this summer." She nodded with a smile that said, "We'll see."

For the rest of the summer my mailing address would be: Postmaster; General Delivery; Klawock, Alaska 99925.

One down, two to go and my next stop was Tongass Traders.

Still standing on the dock where it had been built before the end of the nineteenth century, the store is a Ketchikan landmark. Here you can buy anything from housewares to hoochies (fishing lures).

First floor at the rear of the store: clothing.

I handed the rain gear and red rubber boots to the old man behind the counter. He smiled and said, "Hmm, looks like you're gonna go fish'n?" I nodded, "Commercial."

He smiled, "That'll be one hundred and ten dollars."

With a sigh I pulled the money from my wallet, which had been hemor-rhaging cash at every turn, and handed it over. I pointed to the wall behind the counter. "So what's the story on that patch?"

He looked up at the repair, eight feet above his head, made more than seventy years earlier. Since we were the only two people in his department, he a little bored and in need of a little conversation took the time to explain that during Ketchikan's notorious heyday, the principal mode of travel and commerce was by sail. During that time the narrow Tongass channel was packed with sailing vessels: barques, schooners, windjammers of all descriptions coming and going, all jockeyed for position. It's a well-known fact that such vessels, especially when the wind shifted, were not known for their maneuverability. He said, "Yes sir, that's where a bowsprit came through the wall and that patch's a memento to those sailing ships that lost their steerage while in tight quarters."

While he spoke I could imagine the commotion in Tongass Narrows: sailing ships transporting cannery workers and miners to and from Ketchikan, Seattle, and San Francisco; supply ships on their way to Wrangell, Petersburg, Sitka, and Juneau; freighters moving their cargos of canned and salted salmon along with copper, silver and gold from the mines; government ships and fishing boats. Barely enough room to turn around.

He handed me my items. "Good luck, and stay out of trouble." There's that word again.

I left the store feeling just fine in my shin length red rubber boots that I rolled down to ankle height just like those of any self-respecting fisherman or logger. No need to wear rain gear since the weather had turned from overcast with drizzling rain to cloudless, sunny, and sixty five degrees; two down, one to go. Plenty of time to spare so I took a seat on the edge of the dock.

Here I was in the land of my grandfather just sitting on this dock looking out over Tongass Narrows and wondering about him. I felt a connection with this place. And for a moment I was lost in daydream..

And then, with just a glance in my direction, she brushed by me on her way down the ladder to the boat tied below. Once alight on the deck she disappeared into the cabin. I could still smell her lingering scent. The comforting aroma of the sea was blotted out by that of cheap perfume. "Definitely out of place," I thought.

She was a good looking blonde in a white summer dress and sleeveless low cut top. She was young but not that young. In her thirties I'd guess, but older than her years.

I reached into my pocket and pulled out the sandwich I bought on the ferry. I took a bite; ham and cheese on rye.

"So you wanna get a beer?" It was Ben standing next to me. I guess my attention was on the blonde.

About that time the cabin door opened and the woman in white appeared. Somewhat disheveled she looked almost the same as she did thirty minutes earlier except her blonde hair which had been in a tightly wound bun on the back of her head was now down around her shoulders.

She never looked up at me but simply climbed over the boat's rail onto the deck of the next boat tied alongside. As before, without hesitation she opened the cabin door and disappeared inside.

Ben looked at me and said as a matter of fact, "She's just one of the working girls that follow the summer fleet up here." He paused, "How about a beer?"

I might wonder about the blonde later but not now. Beer was more important. As I turned to leave I donated my sandwich to my audience of seagulls gathered about. The Sourdough Bar and Grill is a fisherman's hangout, a home away from home. It's a dimly lit place. The only frills were the dozens of eight by ten, framed photographs of fishing boats hanging on the walls: fishing boats fishing; fishing boats sinking; fishing boats in dry dock; and fishing boats on the rocks.

Ben and I bellied up to the bar, ordered a couple of drafts and burgers then sat back on our stools.

Jack and Molly McGue ran the place. Jack was the barkeep and Molly the cook (breakfast and lunch but no dinner). They were both in their sixties, over-weight, outspoken, and had been the Sourdough's owner operators for the past twenty years. They were both born and raised in Ketchikan and every fisherman in town knew and trusted the McGues. When they liked you, they liked you. But if they didn't, then you might as well leave their place because you probably wouldn't get served. They had no children of their own but that didn't mean they didn't have dependents. It was quite common for a deck hand to leave his pay with the McGues; if he needed a loan or to be bailed out of jail, he could count on the McGues. And at the end of the season his money was in the safe waiting for him. No need to bother with banks when the McGues were there.

"How's the burger?" Molly asked.

"Best I've had in a long time." I was telling the truth. She looked a Ben, "I like your friend, Benny."

About that time a huge native came through the door. He put his enormous hand on Ben's shoulder. Without waiting for a response he spoke, "Wher've you been, nephew? Long time no see? What, you don't like us anymore?"

Ben turned and they both embraced. Then the big man sat down on the stool next to me.

"Uncle Bobby this is my friend Dylan," Ben paused, "He wants to go fishing with us."

Jack brought Bobby a beer.

The fisherman took a swig. He asked, "So you wanna go fishing with Benny?" Expecting a positive response, I nodded with a smile, "Yes."

Without even the ·slightest interest Bobby said in a matter of fact, almost condescending way, "Lots of guys wanna go fishing."

Bobby turned back to his beer.

My ego deflated, I decided it best not to press the issue and returned to my burger and beer.

Molly stood in front of me and said, "Don't worry about Bobby, he says that to all the white guys."

Bobby's face flushed.

Then he turned to Ben and asked, "How long you gonna to be in town?"

Ben washed the last bite of burger down with a gulp of beer then with a stammer. "Ah, we're catching the Chilkat back to the big island tomorrow."

Bobby placed his hand back on Ben's shoulder and said, slowly and clearly, in his deep raw weather-beaten voice, "Then you better get your butt over to see your auntie Dorothy tonight at dinner if you know what's good for you!"

With that, I "wolfed down" the rest of my burger then changed seats with Bobby. And while the two of them "talked family," I sat with my back propped against the bar, brew in-hand, listening to Country Western coming from the juke box and absorbing the local color. The volume was set on high and Willy Nelson was singing "Bloody Mary Morning." Conversations were loud and eavesdropping was easy.

After another beer I felt at peace.

The thin stubble faced fisherman on the bar stool to my left looked to be in his mid- forties (it's hard to tell, as the weather has a way of aging one prematurely). He wore a bandage over his face from right to left cheek which hid his nose. Actually he had no nose.

"So what the hell happened, Charlie?" asked his friend.

Charlie paused to finish his beer then continued, "You know I love dogs, right?" And Sammie, just sober enough to follow the conversation answered, "Yeah."

Charlie continued, "Well Friday night," he paused, "I was minding my own business just walking home from the Forty Niner and this piece of shit Doberman comes up to me wagging his tail," another pause, "So I bent down and patted him on the head."

Sammie waved Jack over for another round of boilermakers, "So?"

"So, before I could say nice dog, he bit off my nose and ran with it down the street."

"Bit off your nose, holy crap!"

"You're damn right!" Charlie slammed his empty shot glass on the bar and then downed the beer chaser. "Almost caught him but the worst part was, when I was within a hundred yards, he turned, sat down, looked me straight in the eyes and swallowed. My nose, he ate my nose and I think he was smiling while he did it. If I ever meet up with that dog again he'll be halibut bait for sure!"

Sammie asked him, "Are you gonna fish the next opening?"

Charlie seemed a little surprised, "Why not?" And then realized his friend's concern, "No problem, the doc's gonna make me a fake nose!"

The music stopped and they lowered their voices. My attention then turned to a young couple sitting next to the wall and underneath an eight by ten black and white photograph of a seine boat at low tide, grounded "high and dry" on the rocks and suspended ten feet above the water.

A wicker bassinet sat on their table alongside a half dozen or more empty beer bottles. Inside the bassinet, the infant was fast asleep under his blue comforter.

The anxious young mother said, "Johnnie, we've gotta catch the Chilkat in the morning. Let's go back to the hotel."

He slurred. "Okay, okay, don't worry; will ya. Just one more drink and we'll be out a here."

Her drunken husband's answer didn't reassure her. She'd seen him in this condition before. She was tired, and soon her baby would need to be fed and his diaper changed.

Enter the Filipino taxi driver. Without saying a word he looked over at Jack who nodded and then pointed at the young couple's table.

The driver stood three steps behind the woman. "Jack called you a cab, time to go now." At first, the young man was a little reluctant to leave but the driver persisted. "Jack called you a cab, time to go now." He wasn't about to lose his fare.

Jack called over, "Big John, you've had enough to drink and you've got a ferry to catch in the A. M." He added, "I don't want to have to talk to your father about this!"

John struggled to rise from his seat. Had it not been for the support of the little driver, he most likely would have fallen over backward. He looked at Jack, "Okay, okay, sorry, we're going. No need to get mad."

The young woman holding the basket in one hand and her husband with the other smiled at Jack and mouthed the words, "Thank you."

A moment or two later and the four were out the front door and into the waiting checkered taxi.

Soon after, another fisherman entered the bar, walked up to Bobby and whispered something about a birthday present. Bobby turned to Ben and just said, "Gotta go Benny, see you tonight," and added, "You too Dylan."

Shortly after Bobby and the fisherman disappeared out the door an argument broke out at the pool table at the rear of the bar. It was the five fishermen

I met earlier that morning. I was about to stand but Ben's hand on my shoulder kept me down.

Ben said, "That's trouble, Dylan. Maybe another time but we can't miss dinner and we got a ferry to catch in the morning. No excuses." He paused while gulping down the last of his burger and then finishing off his beer, "Let's go!"

So after a quick tour of Ketchikan (the docks, Creek Street boardwalk, Totem Park and the Deer Mountain salmon hatchery) we headed six miles south of town over a gravel road to the Tlingit village of Saxman where his aunt Dorothy and her husband Bobby Thomas lived. To say it was a rough road was a gross understatement. There were so many ruts, that to drive faster than ten miles per hour put one's vehicle and dental work at risk of being shaken apart.

Their house, built at the turn of the century, is a large three story wood frame structure set on a hill overlooking Tongass Narrows. According to native tradition it is an Eagle Clan house, the clan of Bobby's mother. A favorite meeting place where village elders meet, though for that matter it's open to any neighbor.

We entered through the back door into the wet room (the room where all wet rain wear is hung). Without warning, Ben was grabbed from behind by aunt Dorothy. She was an immense woman and Ben's six foot frame seemed to melt into her embrace.

Moments later she set him free to catch his breath. Standing there with a smile on her face and her hands akimbo, she asked in her well-developed but amicable rhetorical style, "So Benny, you finally found a spare moment in your busy schedule to come visit me?"

As for Ben's repartee, "Yes auntie Dorothy, I always have time for you."

Quickly changing the subject he added, "Oh, this is my friend Dylan Templeton. He might go fishing with us. Dylan, this is my auntie Dorothy."

Dorothy looked over at me then back at Ben and asked, "Might?"

"It's up to pop."

I smiled and said, "Glad to meet you Mrs. Thomas." She smiled at me, "Glad to meet you Dylan."

Her upper arms were as large around as my thighs and when she finally took my hand, it too became momentarily lost in her soft grip.

Ben was her favorite nephew as was she his favorite aunt. I felt good to be there and had the feeling auntie Dorothy liked me.

Through the large bay windows of the grand sitting room stretched a panoramic view of Tongass Narrows. From the Red Cedar beams and paneling, a wonderful fragrance permeated the entire house. And all around, the walls were adorned with native artwork (carved masks, paddles, halibut hooks, drums, and paintings). Bobby Thomas smiled and motioned us to take a seat. We obliged.

While children played on the floor, the men sat and talked, and the women were in the kitchen preparing the evening meal. This was a festive night; the last night all would gather together until the end of the fishing season. The conversation was "fishing" or "the politics of fishing."

The old shriveled native across from me talked about the old days. We listened as he lectured.

"Now each year there are fewer and fewer salmon. We depend on salmon. Not too long ago there were many more. We knew how to protect our salmon. We made our own laws, not white man's laws. There was no Department of Fish and Game to tell us what we could and could not do. We knew what must be done. We had our own guards to protect the spawning grounds and streams; that was their responsibility. And there were so many fish then, that we could fish when we wanted. We had fish traps. There were many canneries. Today all has changed. Now we are told what to do by the government."

Everyone in that room was a commercial seiner (net fisherman). One after the other, the elders spoke about how it was years ago. Others talked about how hard it had become to make a living and their optimistic hopes for the coming season.

Besides Ben there were just two individuals in that room not from Saxman. Myself and a young fisherman from Seattle; Barry Stahl wasn't much older than me but was well respected by the locals as one who had worked his way up the ladder. He began as a "bare bones" hand troller (hook and line) and fished just about every fishery in southeast by himself from an eighteen foot skiff to eventually become a "high line seiner," consistently catching more than a hundred thousand salmon each season.

He owned and operated, The Harvester, a sleek new white and blue trimmed fifty five foot fiberglass seiner. She was fast, clean, and comfortable, and Barry was known throughout southeast Alaska to be a fair and honest skipper who said what he thought and hired local fishermen. He was accepted by the community.

Plus he was engaged to be married to Angie Thomas; Bobby and Dorothy's oldest daughter.

Bobby, just to "stir the pot," turned to Barry and asked him what he thought about what was just said.

Barry, knowing he was on thin ice, took a deep breath, paused then said, "Okay here it is. I've listened to each of you speak your minds and I think you're missing the point." He had everyone's attention.

"The point is, there are fewer fish today because of what was done years ago. It's all about the money, then and now. There was no management then. Fish traps, no fishing limits, canneries, crooked politicians. They all took a toll. And add to that, herring are now caught by the thousands of tons and sold to the Japanese. They are the primary feed for salmon and without them there will be no salmon. As I said, it's all about the money."

The audience was quiet, without emotion. As Bobby rose to leave the room I think I was the only one to see a slight smile cross his face.

It seemed as if no one was interested in what Barry said. No one spoke. Then another elder turned to him and said, "We do what we must to survive."

The elders shook their heads in agreement. And that was the end of that.

Another cousin of Ben's said, "Last year I fired two deck hands because of drugs.

It used to be booze, then grass, and now cocaine. God forbid another Saint Paul." At that point a young girl standing in the doorway announced, "dinner's ready."

We took our places at the large oak planked table, well-worn from a hundred years of use. Ben and I sat on either side of auntie Dorothy. Bobby sat at the head of the table. Heads bowed, Dorothy delivered a short prayer asking for protection and guidance for these fishers through the coming season.

It was the traditional Tlingit meal held at the beginning and end of each salmon season.

The platters were heaped with barbecued salmon steaks and heads, salted salmon caviar, halibut, abalone, king crab, shrimp, sea cucumber, smoked seal, candle fish, black cod, beach asparagus, herring row on kelp, soap berries, rice, and more.

The food was passed around and everyone, including myself, helped themselves. I've never been accused of being a picky eater. Everything was delicious.

Except (in my opinion) for that smoked seal meat. It came from a seal killed in fresh water during the late fall when salmon were spawning. The meat had a strong almost rancid flavor which, try as I might, I could not get past my lips. Fortunately for me no one seemed to notice as I passed my portion to Rocky the Tabby cat waiting patiently at my feet.

Oolakan (candle fish), stink eggs, and smoked seal meat. To this day I've never acquired the taste for any of them. It's a cultural thing.

Dinner conversation was light: quality of the food, fishing, a smattering of local politics, price of salmon, and gossip.

The last remaining delicacy on my plate was the herring eggs: pieces of kelp (sea weed) covered with the little translucent eggs (smaller than grains of rice) and served after being blanched in boiling water for just a few seconds. They had the salty taste of the ocean and the texture of pencil erasers. Not bad from my perspective, but nothing to write home about.

Raymond, the seven year old sitting next to me, tugged on my shirt sleeve and whispered with a slight lisp, "I belong to the Dog Salmon clan."

"Dog Salmon," I asked. Everyone's attention was directed at us.

"Yep, Dog Salmon, they're the ones with big teeth and when we catch them they get tangled in the nets."

"Oh," I said, "you must be a fisherman."

"Yep," he said as he sat straighter in his chair.

Smiles appeared around the table.

Another budding pescador, not to be outdone by Raymond, announced, "Dog Salmon is another name for Chum Salmon." All around the table were more smiles and nodding heads.

In short order I learned from these two that Dog Salmon were used by the Eskimos as dog food. That they made excellent halibut bait (better than octopus) and were especially good for smoking (Raymond's favorite were Hawaiian Strips). And their skin can be tanned into leather.

Ben turned to me and said, "Wait till you have to untangle the big males from the net. You're gonna hate them by the end of summer."

Try as we might, the fifteen of us could not consume all the food at that table. At one point, Dorothy asked what brought me to Alaska.

This was the first time that night that the guests seemed interested in what I was about to say. Years later I would explain that in my opinion, around outsiders native villagers are a shy people. Their shyness is easily mistaken for indifference or even downright hostility. And nothing could be further from the truth.

I answered, "Well, I grew up in California. I never knew my grandfather. He died before I was born, but my mother told me he was from somewhere in southeast Alaska. She wasn't sure exactly where but she thought it might have been near Sitka. He was an Alaskan native. Tlingit, she thought. Both of his parents died of Tuberculosis when he was a little boy and the church sent him and his two brothers to boarding school. The boys were adopted by different families and somehow he ended up in Kansas. My mother died five years ago and for as long as I can remember, I've wanted to come to Alaska to find something of my past. So here I am."

Aunt Dorothy put a reassuring hand on my shoulder and from that instant I felt like I belonged. For the rest of the evening I was a included in conversations. I even noticed Dorothy's eldest daughter Sissy, who previously showed no interest whatsoever in my presence, glancing more often in my direction. There was just something about her, maybe it was her smile, that made me feel a little lightheaded.

There was just something.

That most satisfying evening eventually wore to a close. Hugs, handshakes, and wishes for a prosperous season. After the last of the other guests, "stuffed to the gills," left, Ben and I helped clear the table. Then Ben put his arm around his aunt and said, "We've gotta go. We got a ferry to catch in the morning."

She forced a smile and then he asked, "Auntie Dorothy, when ya coming home," and added, "If you ever get tired of Saxman remember everyone misses you in Klawock. It's been a long time since you visited."

A smile crossed her face. She glanced at Bobby then back to Ben, "Maybe this month, Benny. Angie will be working at the cannery and Sissy will be fishing with her dad so that might be a good time."

In deference, she looked over to Bobby who agreed and offered, "There's gonna be at least three or four purse seine openings off the west coast this summer. We'll be there." he added, "You boys are welcome to stay here tonight or on the boat if you want."

3

ALASKA ROSE

On the drive back to Ketchikan after a night of general gluttony, that same well-worn gravel road we traveled earlier had lost none of its charm. As we bumped and rattled along, potholes I previously ignored now brought the after-taste of seal meat and fish eggs back to my palate. Needless to say, it was a definite relief to leave the gravel and reach the asphalt. The tempest within my stomach began to calm.

"You okay?" Ben asked.

"Sure. Why?"

"Just asking, you look a little pale."

"Musta been something I ate."

I changed the subject. "Ben, what's the story of the Saint Paul?"

"Well," he paused, "one night at the end of last summer the Richardson family was murdered aboard their seiner, the Saint Paul. They found the boat on the back side of Fish Egg Island burned to the water line but still floating. The skipper Jim, his wife Linda, their two boys and a greenhorn deckhand were all tied up and then shot."

"Why." I asked.

"No one really knows. But the rumor is drugs."

"Drugs;" the plot thickened.

"Yep, the story is the greenhorn was dealing drugs, big time; to the rest of the fleet. It's easy to get drugs during the fishing season. People make a lot of money fishing and lots of drugs are bought and sold. Anyway, rumor is the deck-hand ripped off drugs from his suppliers in Seattle which pissed them off, so they sent people up here to hunt him down. They found him one night when the Saint Paul was tied up to the dock in Craig. They killed him and everyone aboard and then set the Saint Paul on fire to sink the evidence. But it had too much flotation to sink. At the time, no one thought much about the Saint Paul leaving the dock in the middle of the night and they probably never will figure out what happen for sure. There has been an arrest and a trial but no conviction."

It was midnight and just a hint of sunset remained by the time we reached the City Dock at the north end of town. It was low tide which meant a drop of twenty feet from street level down a very steep and sometime slippery (wet weather) ramp to Bobby's Alaska Rose. Bits and pieces of asphalt shingles (for added traction) still remained tacked along the length of the ramp; a poignant reminder of the hazards of winter's ice on a steep ramp.

The fifty five foot Alaska Rose was built in 1932. She is a limited entry seiner (only those boats that have a permit to fish commercially are allowed to do so). Planked with Cypress over Yew and Oak ribs, she is designed for heavy weather and in every sense is a true classic. She has a full body flowing aft to a broad tapered stern and can pack fifty tons of iced fish. And although she has been in the Thomas family for four generations and could easily outlast the next four, her future is uncertain. The fact is her kind was built without frills and for one purpose only, to catch fish. The trend over the past five years though has been to replace the wood fleet with more comfortable, faster, and economical fiberglass, aluminum, or steel vessels. Wood however, will persist as long as towns like Klawock, Saxman, Angoon, Kake, Hoonah, Hydaburg, and others throughout southeast Alaska survive.

We were welcomed aboard by Napoleon Dumas, one of Bobby's long time crew members. Apparently, Bobby had called down to the boat earlier to let Napoleon know we were coming.

Friends since childhood, Ben and Napoleon greeted each other as brothers. They fished together over the years on numerous boats under all kinds of conditions and survived whatever Mother Nature threw at them. They both belonged to the brotherhood of Alaskan fishermen who work in the world's most dangerous profession.

Napoleon smiled as he shook my hand and said, "Just call me Nappy," and then motioned the both of us inside. The three of us sat down in the galley. A fresh pot of Nappy's strong black coffee stood on the table next to a half-eaten piece of chocolate cake and a brand new skinning knife decorated with a short piece of red ribbon with a card that read, "For your next deer; happy birthday, Bobby."

He picked the knife up, pulled it out of its sheath, and lightly ran his calloused thumb along its razor sharp edge. Satisfied with the shallow cut he smiled, "Nothing beats a Schrade; lost my old one on last year's deer hunt." He passed it around and said that it was his twenty eighth birthday. He was younger than I would have guessed.

I detected a touch of sadness behind his smile. But then again Nappy was a loner. He was a Tsimpsean native from the town of Metlakatla on Annette Island, about thirty miles south of Ketchikan. It's the only Indian reservation in Alaska. Like all Pacific coast islanders, The Tsimpseans are a seafaring people. A hundred plus years ago they came to Annette Island by canoe from British Columbia with their Anglican pastor, Father Duncan and established their reservation.

His home was the sea and as a commercial fisherman he lived a nomadic life on one boat after the other with different skippers and different crews. In early winter he fished the Bering Sea for King Crab. In the spring he fished Annette Island for herring and then Sitka and Wrangell for Black Cod. Late spring and early summer he fished Bristol Bay for Sockeye Salmon. And for the remainder of summer and the fall, he fished Ketchikan waters and the west coast of Prince of Wales and points north to Sitka for Pinks and Dogs. In between seasons he returned to Metlakatla and his family.

It's hard, often dangerous and lonely work, but Nappy was hooked on it. Sadly, like so many who take to this life, to relieve the pain and boredom he turned to alcohol and drugs. He wasn't just a deck hand. No, on this boat Nappy was also the cook; an excellent cook. On any morning before the rest of the crew were out of their bunks, Nappy would be in the galley working over the cast iron oil stove preparing breakfast. There is a special art to it. Once the stove is lit, the damper is adjusted. If opened too much the stove bums red hot like a blast furnace. Opened too little and the stove will belch forth enough smoke to drive everyone out of the galley.

Nappy was an oil stove wizard and it worked perfectly. The crew was happy. When breakfast was over and the crew out on deck, he'd begin the evening meal, which might be a rice shrimp curry, venison or pork roast, baked salmon, or whatever his choice. Once in the oven the meal slow cooked and simmered for the rest of the day.

During that time Nappy worked alongside the crew to do whatever else necessary to set the net and pull in the catch. Great cooks are a rare find and the galley was Nappy's domain, but once on deck, his butt belonged to the skipper. Oh yes, the rule was never, no never, wear your wet, jelly fish dripping, scale encrusted rain gear into the galley. Nappy had a meat cleaver and nothing is more intimidating than a Tsimpsean cook waving a cleaver and screaming, "Get Out!"

It was well past midnight and I was fighting a losing battle to stay awake. Another cup of coffee had no effect. The last thing I remember before I dozed off was Ben and Nappy exchanging local gossip of no interest to me. Then the next thing I knew, Ben tapped me on the shoulder and said, "it's six o'clock partner, time to get up, we got a ferry to catch." Before I could respond he disappeared out the doorway.

I was in the forecastle (pronounced folks-hole). Can't say whose bunk I slept in or how I got there but it was comfortable. The forecastle is the forward-most compartment below deck and here with four bunks squeezed into the "V" of the bow, is the crew's quarters; and just behind the crew's quarters is the engine room.

At sea the main engine is constantly running and that generates a lot of heat. Added to that is the pervasive smell of diesel throughout. It is an understatement to say, "The forecastle is an uncomfortable and stifling place to sleep." However, the crew is usually so exhausted from setting and resetting the net and working the gear, to them sleep comes easily. Comfort my friend is a luxury left back at the dock.

Did someone say, "Get up." I nearly jumped into my boots and made my way out the door and down the passageway to the galley where the rest of the crew was finishing breakfast. No chit chat. I had just enough time to thank Nappy for his hospitality, wish the crew good fishing, and grab a cup of coffee. With the exception of Nappy, the crew must have thought I was a crazy man.

4

THE CHILKAT

It was a short five minute drive to the ferry terminal where after purchasing our tickets we then became a link in a short chain of cars and trucks, some trailering boats, waiting our turn to "back down" the steep steel boarding ramp to the little Chilkat. Definitely a touch and go experience but significantly easier in summer compared to the icy low tide conditions of winter.

It was a misty morning.

Once at the bottom of the boarding ramp we were funneled over the Chilkat's bow ramp into the belly of the little boat and squeezed into one of its three tight vehicle lanes. The vehicle deck could accommodate anywhere from three to twenty five vehicles (depending on their size).

Right, middle, or left. The choice wasn't ours. It was strictly up to the deckhand in charge. It must be said, backing off the bow ramp into the left or right lanes (port or starboard) is an especially delicate maneuver and seasoned Chilkat voyagers hope for the middle lane. Thanks to Ben's driving ability and the expertise of the crewman directing us, we were directed without mishap, into the starboard lane. Always make sure to fold your side view mirrors in, lest they are knocked off by one of the steel stanchions separating the lanes. Again, it's a real tight fit. Less skilled drivers than Ben had trouble negotiating the obstacle course but within forty five minutes the ferry was packed stem to stern with our caravan of vehicles in final preparation for the trip to Prince of Wales Island (POW).

The ninety foot Chilkat was in cartoon contrast to the Malaspina. The moniker, "the chili dog" comes to mind. Even so, like the rest of the fleet her steel hull was painted blue with gold trim, and she sported a crisp white superstructure. Beside the American ensign she flew the state flag with its eight golden stars: the North Star above seven others framing the constellation Ursa Major (The Big Dipper); all on a field of Navy Blue.

The Chilkat brings to mind, visions of, "The Little Engine That Could."

While her smaller size and bow ramp allowed her to service numerous isolated communities throughout Alaska's panhandle, for which she was well appreciated, passenger comfort was not her "strong suit." The dining rooms, cafeterias, observation decks, solariums, bars, etc. found on larger ferries were not in the Chlkat's design.

With a round bottom, she would roll even in the smallest swell. And to make matters worse, her single steel aft passenger cabin had the feel of a detention cell. In a rolling sea, within this confined poorly ventilated space packed with passengers, seasickness was common. The fetid stench could be so overpowering that when one person became sick, the rest of the crowd often followed suit. The well experienced passenger though, knew it best, if possible, to avoid the cabin and stay outside on deck (weather dependent), or in the little galley (if the crew allowed), or in the wheelhouse (skipper dependent).

We became part of the crowd moving topside, up the stairway from the vehicle deck to the passenger cabin. The steel narrow stairwell echoed our passage. Once at the top we entered the cabin but unlike the settling crowd that jockeyed for seating, Ben and I exited another door onto the outer deck and then up another flight of stairs to the wheelhouse.

We stopped at the doorway and the little bearded man at the wheel turned and motioned us to enter. We were in luck. The captain and Ben were friends. And as only one of the three visitor seats was occupied, we now had the best seats in the house. It was another beautiful morning. The water was calm and quiet.

Seven o'clock. The little Chilkat with its captain, an engineer, three deckhands, and fifty plus passengers, was ready to cast off. I could feel the boat come alive. The noise of steel against steel as the bow ramp was raised and then slammed shut against the hull like a drawbridge; the throb and vibration of the engines. The creaking and groaning of the hull's steel plate; the deck crew barking orders at each other as the heavy hausers were freed from their moorings and hauled aboard. In a moment or two we slid away from the dock and were headed for Prince of Wales Island.

Once underway, Ben introduced me to captain Black. The old man sitting next to me was asleep. Ben looked at him said, "That's Stan Brown," then smiled. "He likes to party late when he comes to town."

The captain asked where I was from. When I told him California, he said, in a deep raspy voice, "I was born there too but been living here in southeast for the past thirty years. Yeah, I've been the Chilkat's skipper for the past twenty years and deck hand ten years before that." He paused. His voice softened, "Gonna retire soon; too much rain."

I asked, "Any plans?"

He stared at the horizon and said, almost in a growl, "I'm sure as hell not gonna go fishing." He paused but kept staring out the window, "Spent most of my life on the water. I'm going somewhere where there ain't no ocean and it don't rain much: Yuma, Arizona or Tucumcari, New Mexico or Aspermont, Texas. Somewhere where the sun shines and there's warm dry ground and there ain't any rubber neck tourists."

Ben looked at Captain Black and said, "You'll be back skipper. This is your home."

A light rain began to fall. The captain turned from the wheel. "Too many changes for this ol' sea dog; I've been through two wars and two wives. It's not the same as it used to be and a change'll do me good."

At that point the engineer entered the wheelhouse with clipboard in hand and handed the captain a cup of coffee. Their conversation was barely audible. Something about engine performance, keeping an eye on one of the pressure gauges, and securing the car deck. The captain reviewed the paperwork and after turning the last page and finishing his coffee he said, "Okay Scotty, steady as she goes." Without saying another word, he smiled at us and left the wheelhouse.

It's a known fact that on any summer day in southeast Alaska, the wind often blows from every direction. The pattern is similar to a clock moving backwards, counterclockwise. A cool morning will start with the wind from the north. Then as the day warms the wind will shift to the west and later to the south and then to the east. Finally towards sunset, it will have shifted completely around and blow from the north. It is the wind and tide that generates waves and that day was no different. What started out as a calm glassy-smooth thirty minute trip up Tongass Narrows developed into a two hour, fifteen mile roller coaster ride across Clarence Strait.

The jagged snow-capped mountains of Prince of Wales Island were visible from the start; geological newcomers. As we pitched and rolled, and rolled and pitched, the taste of smoked seal meat returned. At that point, I'm not saying I was sick, I was just a little on edge but I knew enough to keep my eyes pinned on those unmoving peaks. A rock solid antidote (most of the time) for sea sickness; it's common knowledge among seamen, that in a rolling sea it's best to focus on something stationary. The horizon or mountain peaks both qualify.

While Ben went below for a cup of coffee and a visit with family (he seemed to have family everywhere we went), I was content to stay put and watch the scenery. To our port side, we passed that smart little Valnar lighthouse which marked the reef for which it was named. It's a reassuring beacon always signaling safe passage through the northwest entrance to Tongass Narrows. Grateful I was where I was and not packed into that steel aft cabin with the other fifty plus passengers.

A pod of Gray Whales moving due north crossed our bow. As they disappeared into the distance, I became lost in daydream; the smell of the sea and salt air, the peaceful roll of the ocean, and those gliding calling gulls. They all contributed.

Three quarters of the way across Clarence Straight the old man beside me broke the peace. All of a sudden he sat up and pointed forward out the window, "I used to do a lot of hand trolling for kings (king salmon) just off that little island."

I tried but just couldn't see at what he was pointing. At its distance from us, Prince of Wales Island appeared in one dimensional profile as a dark form on the horizon without any detail and the many smaller islands that lay just off its shore were lost in shadow.

Soon though, Kasaan Peninsula, which marked our course direction, came into view as did the forest outline, then individual trees, and then the beach, and then more and more detail. Almost impatient with me he repeated, "That's it there, Grindall Island."

It's just another tiny island at a distance of about a half mile or so from the tip of the headland. Barely visible at first, I had to squint to see it but then finally, with a certain degree of pride I exclaimed, "There it is, Grindall Island." He smiled.

Stan began to talk, "Yes sir, I caught a lot of King Salmon there. Didn't make too much money fishing in those days though; worked a lot of other jobs to raise a family then."

Not to interrupt, I nodded in agreement.

He continued, "I was born and raised in Metlakatla. It was a good place for a boy to grow up; deep bays, high mountains and plenty of fish and game. When the old cannery burned down in Chester Bay, I helped build a new one. I helped build the dam on top of Purple Mountain. I (with pride) was a carpenter and a pipe fitter and an electrician."

He went on, "Every year when the salmon returned, school was out. We all worked at the cannery; men, women, and children. That was our way of life. Our fish traps caught a lot of salmon. We still use the traps. The white man's are gone; outlawed."

He added, "We built a cold storage and freezer."

Stan is the second Tsimpsean I had met and remains one of my favorites.

Like villages throughout southeast Alaska, then and to a lesser extent today, life in Metlakatla centered on the cannery and sawmill; the sawmill provided lumber for construction, and scrap wood to fuel the boilers which produced the steam which turned the turbines to make electricity to run the cannery and light the town.

He doesn't fish anymore. But Stan is an artist, renowned for his southeast native carvings. And always, he remains true to his heritage.

5

PRINCE OF WALES ISLAND

After four hours of bobbing and weaving we crossed Clarence Straight and entered Kasaan Bay. The tide had changed and the water calmed. About seven miles up the bay on our starboard side we passed a small native village. Stan pointed and said, "There! That's Kasaan." He paused and then continued, "The Haida moved there over a hundred years ago from Old Kasaan (now deserted and in ruin on Skowl Ann at the head of the bay). That was the home of Chief Skowl."

"Chief Skowl?" I asked.

Stan said, "Yes, he was a fierce Kaigani Haida chief from the Queen Charlotte Islands. He sent raiding parties as far away as Seattle; took lots of prisoners. They became slaves or dinner or both. Chief Seattle said, and it is in stone, "it is better to surrender to the white man than suffer the wrath of the Haida."

Scotty, who up to that time had been silent, turned from the wheel and added, "He had an adopted daughter (Mary) who married a stowaway off a whaling ship. His name was Baronovitch or something like that. As a wedding present, the chief gave the couple the Karta River and all its salmon.

Scotty pointed up ahead, "There, that's Karta Bay, you can't see it from here but the river is just behind that bend. They salted salmon there and sold them to the Russians, English, and Americans. But, Baronovitch had a greedy side. Even though his trading post was successful, he decided to steal otter pelts from his father-in-law and sell them to the Russians. That was a bad idea. Chief Skowl caught him and would have killed him had not Mary intervened. She was pregnant with the chief's first grandson so he let Baronovitch live. Before he died, Baranovitch owned a saltery, trading post, copper mine, and fathered fourteen children. After his death Mary leased the Karta River to the Cutting Packing Company at Loring, just around the comer from Ketchikan), until the Alaska Packers Association stole it from her."

I said, "You sound like you know a lot about Kasaan's history."

Scotty smiled, "Thanks. My brother is a research assistant for the Tongass Historical Society. He loves his work and every time I come home he gives me a history lesson."

At one time Kasaan village had a cannery, dry goods store, restaurant copper mine, fishing fleet, post office, restaurant, saltery, sawmill, and a school (grades one thru eight). But in just a few years after the mine began, it went broke. The cannery burnt down (was rebuilt a number of times). And almost everyone moved away. Still remaining is the school, the general store, and remnants of their fishing fleet.

But as the fleet has aged and the salmon have all but disappeared, Kasaan like many remote villages has turned to its only remaining resource, timber. It is only a matter of time and that too will be gone.

Ben returned to the wheelhouse and took his seat. Pointing forward he said, "We're almost there; just around that point."

We came to the end of Kasaan Bay and finally turned south into Twelvemile Arm. Twenty minutes later we arrived at the ferry terminal. Scotty picked up the microphone and announced our arrival, "Hollis Terminal folks."

I turned to Stan and said, "I enjoyed our talk." He smiled, "Me too."

Ben volunteered, "Need a ride Stan?"

The little terminal was not much more than the end of the gravel highway. No buildings. Just a place where people parked their vehicles, purchased their tickets from a fellow in his van, and waited for the ferry.

Not long after we disembarked the Chilkat we turned off the main highway onto a narrow dirt road. It wound through the forest to a peaceful little bay at the head of Twelve Mile Arm and then along the beach for about a half mile or so. During the summer months the road is passable but during the high tides of winter the road is under water.

At the turn of the twentieth century Hollis was a productive gold and silver mining town (population 1000). Remnants of that era lay scattered throughout the forest. Now the town is just a collection of cabins and houses and memories (but that's another story).

After dropping Stan off at his cabin we caught up with the caravan and took our place at the end of the line behind a slow moving motor home towing a skiff packed to the gunnels with camping gear. Tourists I guessed. Then, barely five minutes later, without warning, Ben slammed on his brakes and we slid to a halt on the gravel barely missing a sow black bear and her two cubs as they sauntered leisurely across the road. As we waited we watched the skiffs stern disappear over the next hill.

The single lane road wound for twenty five miles through the mountains to the west side of the island. Centuries old pristine cedar and spruce forests; cascading waterfalls off sheer slopes; wild game and a minimum of humanity; pure and unadulterated beauty.

Forty five minutes later and almost to our destination, we passed by a shiny new log truck, unburdened by load and parked by the side of Klawock Lake.

I'm not sure why, but for a moment after looking at that idling truck with the lake and virgin forest in the background, I had an uneasy feeling in the pit of my stomach; could've been a premonition of things to come or just the seal meat again.

Ben broke the silence, "That's the future Dylan."

Another mile or so and the road forked. West to Klawock and south to Craig; we turned west.

6

KLAWOCK

It was another one of those rare sunny summer days. The town is just off the main road and strung out for about a mile or so along its bay. Pretty much unchanged over the past two hundred plus years. A few houses (some abandoned), post office, school, sawmill, cannery, and a cemetery. Originally this place was a southern summer camp for the Tlingit who wintered twenty miles to the north on Tuxekan Island. Fishing was good here; and here Tlingits caught, smoked, dried, and salted their winter supply of salmon.

The five mile per hour speed limit is fast enough for the single lane dirt road. As the road took a turn an old abandoned weather-beaten wood framed building that looked as if it was ready to collapse caught my eye. I said, nodding in its direction, "Ya think it'll make it through the next storm?"

Ben looked at me and smiled, "Maybe. That's the old saltery building; a landmark; been here for the past eighty years or so." The original building was built farther up the bay over a hundred years ago. It burned down and was rebuilt. It burned down again and was rebuilt here. It'll either fall down or burn down again but I don't think it'll ever be rebuilt."

In this part of the world, summer is a busy season but life moves at a more or less relaxed pace; children and dogs everywhere. The docks are a center of activity. Fishermen work on their gear, and boats come and go. Old men stood at the railings and watch the activity. Younger men in plywood skiffs motor out to the middle of the bay and set their seines to catch sockeye. An old man points and excitedly yells, "Jumps, jumps." I look and see a salmon leap three feet out of the water; followed by another; then another; like popcorn. It's summer and the red salmon have returned.

We drive to the end of the road and park in front of the largest building in town. The sign above the entrance reads, "Klawock Cannery; first cannery in Alaska; est. 1878." Like the original saltery, the original cannery had burnt to the ground and was then rebuilt. But unlike the sad little building at the other end of town, this building is alive and well.

I follow Ben inside. It's another world. Rushing here and there are cannery workers everywhere. With lots to do and little time to spare, the atmosphere is like that of a bee hive. The three month salmon season will soon be upon them and they push to be ready. If they aren't, that will be costly.

The cannery is an oversized two story barn. All rough cut lumber. Huge spruce beams for support and Douglas Fir plank decking worn to a luster (a result of years and years of countless foot traffic). And special purpose devices everywhere that produce thousands and thousands and thousands of cans of salmon. In the vernacular: machines for butchering; filling; packing; topping; soldering; and cooking.

Someone yells, "Watch it!" And I narrowly escape being run over by a fork lift moving cases of empty cans.

Ben shakes his head, "Gotta be careful around here." I smile, "Sorry about that."

We make our way to the opposite end of the building overlooking the bay. The double doors are open and we walk outside onto the deck. Two seine boats are tied up to the dock opposite us. Ben explained, "in a week or so, this place will be packed with boats delivering fish, cannery workers, and fishermen. The town will come alive."

Just then two of the crewmen off the Mary Ann walk up. Both are native. One Tlingit, the other Eskimo. At well over six feet, this Tlingit is the tallest of us all. His name is "Too Tall."

Ben said, "This here is Dylan Templeton; he wants to fish with us." Too Tall shook my hand, "Glad to meet you Dylan."

Throughout, the short stocky Eskimo never showing any emotion (just like Bobby the first time I met him) or saying a word. Ben introduced him as "Double Shot."

He looked at me and just shook his head in disgust then turned and walked away. I could feel the ice crystals in the air.

Too Tall said, "Don't worry about him. He does that to all white men." Then he turned to Ben and asked, "Did you get everything?"

Ben smiled, "Yep, in the truck."

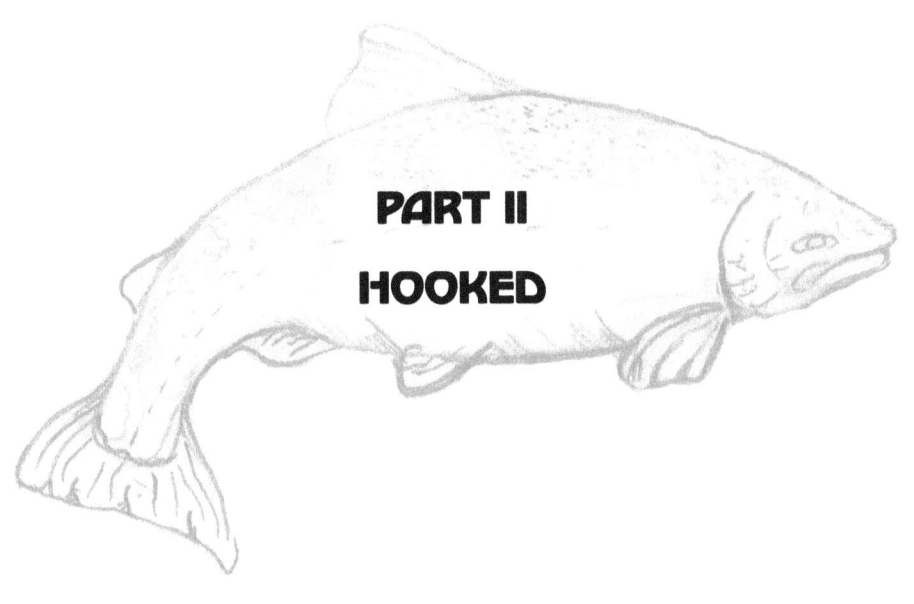

PART II
HOOKED

7

DECK HAND

We stepped through the doorway into the wheelhouse where Ben's father was bent over one of the electronic consoles. The odor of fresh paint and varnish hung in the air.

Ben made the introduction. "Pop, this is Dylan Templeton."

Without looking up the Marvin asked, "You know anything about chart machines?"

"No sir, I don't."

"Too bad; just bought this Decca last year and it's already on the bum; paid twelve thousand dollars for it. I called the company in Seattle and they're sending someone up here tomorrow to fix it."

Age and loss of flexibility go hand in hand. With some difficulty he pushed himself up and free of the machine. Then he smiled, "Getting a little too old for this stuff. So Dylan, Ben tells me you'd like to come an' fish with us?"

I just said, "Yes sir I would."

He fanned the pungent air. "The smell's a little too strong in here," then motioned us to the galley for a cup of Too Tall's coffee.

Marvin had been fishing the Mary Ann for the past forty years. He knew southeast waters like the back of his hand. Well enough to raise a family even in the hardest of times. He could always find fish and in his prime Marvin ruled the deck with an iron fist. On the Mary Ann, there was only one way to fish, and that was Marvin's way.

It is a well-known fact that commercial fishing is, in general, a young man's work.

Although Marvin was no longer physically fit to run the deck (Ben did that), his job was to find the fish and leave the heavy work to the crew. It's true that his disposition had mellowed with age but given the right circumstance, the old lion still knew how to roar. And like his father before him, he would pass the wheel over to his son.

Ben poured the coffee and then excused himself from the galley to join the crew on deck.

Marvin sat silent seemingly lost in thought, then he took a long swig and asked if I'd ever done any commercial fishing before.

I told him I didn't but would like to learn. My straightforwardness seemed to please him.

He asked: where I was raised; my age; my education; military service; what kind of work had I done; what I wanted to do with my life; and if I'd ever been in jail.

I kept my answers short and to the point. Northern California; twenty four; high school; navy; family vineyard; haven't decided; and, no.

With each answer he'd take a sip of coffee and pause briefly before asking the next question.

And that was it. The interview was over. During a long pause he sat without saying a word. Just looking at me; sizing me up. He poured himself another cup of coffee.

I thought to myself, "I should've said more and tried to sell myself; something." He held out his hand and smiled. "You're hired."

I took his hand and thanked him.

I was hired. Yep, I'd receive one share of the gross profit. The skipper, the boat, the net, and each of the crew would each receive a share. The Mary Ann would be my new home for the next three months and I was going to be a real commercial fisherman. Marvin liked me.

Without another word Marvin rose from his seat and, coffee mug in- hand headed back to the wheelhouse.

Ben and Too Tall were on the back deck waiting for me. They both smiled as I approached.

I said, "Well, looks like I'm going to go fishing with you guys."

At that point, they grabbed me, shook my hand, and slapped me on the back. At one time they'd been in my shoes, so any attempt I made to appear cool and calm was doomed to fail.

Ben said, "Congratulations recruit. Don't worry we'll teach you everything you need to know. Just do what you're told and it'll all work out."

Too Tall added, "Someday you might even become a greenhorn."

Marvin emerged from the wheelhouse. "Well boys, Fish and Game made the announcement. We better get ready for Friday's opening. We'll be leaving tomorrow afternoon." With that he left the boat.

Home sweet home; I went below to stow my gear under the forward most bunk (mine) which was squeezed into the "v" of the bow in that tight eight by ten foot forecastle. Our only fresh air came down through the hatch leading to the wheelhouse and was circulated by a little plastic fan which sat on a shelf above my bunk. The compartment being below the water line with only one way in and one way out was no place for the claustrophobic.

My back was turned when the hatch slammed shut. Standing straight up I smacked my head on the shelf; sudden pain. I swore aloud. There was no good reason to shut that hatch especially with someone below. I thought, maybe the boat was haunted. The ghost of some unfortunate sailor washed overboard in a storm and drowned. I finished stowing my gear and made a quick exit.

I took my seat in the galley along with Ben, Too Tall, and Double Shot who stared at me with the slightest grin. Not necessarily friendly. I returned a smile and thought, "Here is our ghost."

Dinner was served. On this boat, Too Tall doubled as cook and deck hand. Like Nappy, Too Tall had his rules but unlike Nappy he didn't need a meat cleaver. He was a big man. One rule was, there would be no alcohol on the boat. But since this was a special occasion to celebrate the beginning of a new season and the hiring of a new deck hand (me), a case of "Ole" had been brought aboard.

For most of the evening I sat and listened to fish stories. With dinner finished, the night still young, and the last of the beer gone, someone suggested we pay a visit to Craig's Inn; a fisherman's bar just seven miles down the road in Craig.

I was tired and sleep would have come easy, but I was part of the crew now and felt compelled to follow along. Anyway, it wouldn't be right if I abandoned my shipmates.

8

CRAIG'S INN

Craig, Alaska is just another sleepy little southeast Alaska town of approximately a thousand people. The economy here is fishing, logging, and booze. It is common knowledge that when sober, commercial fishermen and loggers barely tolerate each other, but when drunk, well let's just say, the alcohol removes that thin veneer of civilization and what's exposed is wrapped in ego and testosterone.

Loggers work six days a week and rest on Sundays. And fishermen rest whenever they are not permitted to fish (the Department of Fish and Game regulates the fishing season). On any night though, both can be found in the bars.

Craig's Inn was open from five to five and as usual the place was packed. A familiar voice called us over. It was Stan Brown. One would think, a bar is a bad place for a recovering alcoholic, but Stan loved to dance and had changed his drink to coffee; strong black coffee. The bartenders always kept a fresh pot on the warmer for Stan.

He didn't own a car but since he was usually the only sober soul in the house, friends gladly handed him their keys and he'd drive them home.

Stan took a swig of his coffee. He said, "Not too many women here tonight but the band's good."

I'm not so sure about the band but he was right about the women. I counted five and they weren't alone. Live loud country-western music and the place, packed with loggers and fishermen were doing their best to drink themselves unconscious. The ratio of men to women was twenty to one.

A few more drinks and I wasn't sure who said what, but whatever it was resulted in a drag out, "down and dirty" brawl which involved beer bottles and pool cues. Too Tall ended up on the floor, flat on his back. Before the police arrived Ben and I pulled him out the back door to Ben's truck where we waited for Double Shot.

I asked, "Where's Double Shot?"

Ben didn't seem overly concerned, "Last time I saw him he was at the bar buying drinks for a red head."

Too Tall moaned and collapsed into the back seat. Then Ben said, "We might as well head back to the boat. Don't worry about Double Shot. He's done this before."

Neither Ben or I and certainly not Too Tall were in any shape to drive back to Klawock.

"Need a driver, boys?" It was Stan Brown. We grinned and shook our heads yes.

On the drive back I said, "I don't think Double Shot likes me."

Ben smiled. "That's nothing new."

"What ya mean by that?"

Ben, calmly and as a matter of fact stated, "He hates all white men." Too Tall tried to sit up, groaned and fell back into his stupor.

I asked, "Why's that?"

Just then a doe wandered in front of us. Stan pulled the wheel to the left; just barely grazing her on the left side of the truck. He calmly brought us back on course.

I looked back to see the little deer leap into the forest and said, "I'm glad you're driving Stan."

He whispered, "Me too. Hit one once and tore up my car real bad. That was the last car I ever owned; too many deer."

All was dark and quiet. The road wound through the dense forest. Only Stan and I were awake.

Stan said, "Dylan, I'll tell you why Double Shot is the way he is," he paused, "He was born in one of the Eskimo villages up north around Nome. When he was just a little boy the government took him from his village. In those days, they took village children and put them in the government school in Sitka; to teach them to be white."

I asked, "So what happened?"

"They thought they were going to make him into a white man but they couldn't. They would punish the children for speaking their Aleut. But no matter what they did to Double Shot he stayed Eskimo. The more they punished him, the more he hated them and still does."

I asked, "So what about the red head tonight?"

Stan said, "Well, I said he hated white men but I didn't say anything about white women. He loves them. He's even got three or four kids by white women."

I said with a touch of sarcasm, "Double Shot is in his sixties, he's short, fat, and missing a couple front teeth. Doesn't sound like a ladies man to me."

Stan laughed. "Ah but that's where you're wrong. That good looking thirty year old red head came into the bar with her young logger boyfriend and she left with Double Shot. And her boyfriend was left holding the bill. I'd say Double Shot understands women well enough."

I thought to myself, Stan understands them too. Even on a night like tonight, with the odds stacked against him, his dance card was filled.

The Decca man came later that morning and fixed the chart plotter. And by the time we were ready to shove off, Double Shot arrived, hung over but with a smile on his face.

9

THE BLESSING OF THE FLEET

It was a beautiful sunny day. We took our place in line in a procession of thirty purse seiners in front of Klawock's cannery. It was "The Blessing of The Fleet;" a ceremony sacred among commercial fishermen everywhere; a day of prayer and memorial for all seafarers; a day to honor those lost at sea and to give strength and guidance for those to carry on.

All heads were bowed while Bishop John of the Catholic Diocese of Juneau stood on the cannery's dock, with the fleet below, and delivered the prayer. As each boat passed by, the priest said a few words and then sprinkled holy water over the vessel.

He was old and frail and few could hear his words but these fishermen had been through the ceremony enough times in the past to know the prayer and routine by heart. There wasn't a fisherman there that hadn't lost a friend or family member to the sea."

Too Tall explained, "Oh, it's just like, when the band plays the Star Spangled Banner before a ball game. Everyone stands and listens, but is chomping at the bit for the game to begin."

10

PRACTICE MAKES PERFECT

This was our "shake down" day. A day of practice; crews set their nets; reset them; and set them again and again until they have "worked out the bugs." If mistakes are to be made, here in sheltered water is the place and time to make and correct them. Coordination is the goal and with enough practice the five man crew will act as one. They will become a well- tuned fishing machine, ready to perform even in the roughest seas: the "outside" waters.

It was "monkey see monkey do." Ben and Too Tall would show me how things were done.

Then I tried. I'd ask, "How's that?"

And they would answer, "Nope."

Then they would show me again and I would do it again and again, until they were satisfied. The pressure was on and no matter how well I thought I did, they would say, move it recruit, faster, faster. Every man had his job and had to anticipate what came next. Aboard a seiner, things happen fast. If they took one step to do a task, I took three (common among recruits). Somehow I managed to satisfy my taskmasters and finally had their seal of approval.

The skipper came out on deck and said, "Okay boys that's good enough," and then he headed the Mary Ann back to Klawock.

By the end of that day, although was I dog tired I felt a sense of accomplishment and belonging. It was a good feeling. Too Tall had a pot of stew on the stove.

It was almost midnight when we tied up to the dock in Klawock. Before leaving the boat Marvin announced, "Get some sleep boys. Tomorrow we're gonna fish Addington." Ben looked over at me; smiled and mouthed the words, "Outside waters."

Within moments after lying down on my bunk, I fell asleep. It could have been a bed of nails and I still would have slept like a rock.

11

HEADING WEST

The next morning we took on a load of ice and headed west for Noyes Island. It was a grand and glorious day. Just a slight breeze rippled the calm water. We cruised past one island and then another; up one channel and down the next. By the time we reached the Gulf of Esquibel it was mid-afternoon and we were bucking a fifty knot wind blowing directly at us from the northwest; just another day in southeast Alaska. Thankfully though, after twenty five miles of pitching and rolling, we reached the island and tied up for the night at the old cannery dock in Steamboat Bay; truly a "port in the storm."

The wind can be screaming up or down the channel but here in this protected sanctuary, all is calm. Here in the notorious Steamboat Bay.

The cannery built here at the turn of the century is now just a shell of its former self. It stands all but abandoned now. Run down yes, but at one time it was the pride of the industry;   nested here, beneath Noyes Peak and smack dab in the middle of premier salmon territory. Fish caught here are in prime condition and therefore fetch the highest price. It would seem the perfect place for a cannery. It is another incredibly wild place.

When we arrived there were about thirty other seiners anchored out in the bay or rafted together and tied to the cannery float below its dock. We tied onto the end of a short column of four other boats.

By the end of the day there must have been fifty boats moored for the night waiting for the next day's first salmon opening of the season. It was a reunion of sorts; a time to rekindle old friendships and catch up on gossip.

Professional fishermen follow the fish and as one season ends another one opens somewhere else. Kinda like Bedouins or Gypsies. No matter where the tide takes them, they are drawn back to the same place to start the cycle over again. Familiar faces, a little older, and a little more weather worn; old friends sharing new adventures.

After securing our lines, Too Tall looked over at Marvin and said, "Skipper, me and Double Shot gots some business to take care of. We'll be back later." They climbed over the rail and disappeared across the decks of the other boats and onto the cannery dock.

Ben was busy in the wheelhouse and Marvin and I were in the galley. The coffee was good.

I've always been interested in old abandoned buildings. They have a history all their own. I asked, "So skipper, what's the story here?"

He smiled, poured himself a cup, took a sip and said, "This was a busy place at one time. Back in the thirties, my father delivered fish here. Lots of Chinese workers then; labor was cheap; long hours." He took another sip. "The steamship Astoria would bring them in, every spring from San Francisco and then in the fall after the season was over and the place buttoned up, they'd go back with their cargo of canned salmon. They packed thousands of cases here and the cannery ran for forty years or more."

I asked, "What happened?"

"The Salmon Packers Union burned it down. That's what happened." That perked me up. "Burned it down?"

He continued, "It's complicated. You see, the cannery was owned and run by the Hamlin family who, originally from Klawock had moved back up here from Seattle and ran this place forty years until all hell broke loose." He paused.

I sat back in my seat and waited. Ben walked in, sat down, and poured himself a cup. Marvin continued, "Well you see, like I said, the Hamlin's roots were here in southeast. After the cannery in Klawock had been in business for ten years or so, the Hamlins moved here (from Seattle) and built this one. Yep, for about forty years or so they did real well. Then the mobsters that ran the Salmon Packer's Union paid them a visit and wanted a kickback. The family refused so one night the Union's enforcers burned the place down to the ground. The Hamlins were stubborn though. They rebuilt the cannery and the Union burned it down again."

I asked, "So wasn't there anything they could do?"

"Not a thing. In those days the government was on the Union's side. Anyway the Hamlins rebuilt it one more time but no bank (union pressure) would loan them the money they needed to run it. No payroll, no cannery, case closed. And so the Hamlins moved back to Seattle. It's been sold and resold over and over again but it just cost too much to run. So here it sits."

"That's too bad."

Marvin shook his head, "I agree." Then added, " They sell fuel and ice here now."

Ben chimed in, "Drugs too."

Just then a familiar voice called out from the deck, "Anybody home?"

Ben disappeared out the galley door to investigate. I thought someday I'd write about places like this one. Places only infrequently visited and unknown to most.

Sissy Thomas stuck her head into the galley. "Hi, just thought you might like a little company."

Barry, Angie, and Sissy entered. Ben followed. To say the least, the galley was crowded but we all found a place at the table.

Barry brought a bottle of red wine. Paper cups were passed around and filled. And everyone toasted to their health and success. The wine was full bodied and smooth.

Ben with a smirk remarked, "hmm' Barry, looks like ya decided to switch to a female crew."

Barry calmly replied, "No, it's not all female. Still got a couple of guys; we picked up a new recruit. He's from Seattle; name's John Geeser."

Angie took hold of Barry's arm and said, "I quit my job at the cannery to go fishing with my man," and then held out her left hand to expose her diamond engagement ring.

She laughed, "It's just big enough to keep the girls away."

Sissy looked at Ben and said, "Uncle Gordon came up from Seattle and wanted to fish this summer." A little smile crossed her face. "I let him take my spot with pop so I could be with Angie." She flashed a sheepish grin at me and smiled.

Marvin added, "No need to make excuses for the girls Barry. They're as good as any fisherman in the fleet."

The girls chimed back, "thanks uncle."

Too Tall, back on board, slipped through the doorway and announced, "I've got a roast in the oven."

Sissy said, "We know, we could smell it aboard the Harvester."

Angie followed up, "Umm, that delicious aroma has probably drifted back to Klawock."

Without hesitation (we were half starved), we grabbed our plates.

David James, another one of Barry's crew, joined us. He was one of the James' boys and had fished over the years on a regular basis with both Barry and Marvin. (He had the scars to prove it.)

As they ate, Ben turned to David, "We missed you last season."

"Yeah, thought I'd try catching tuna off California."

Too Tall swallowed his bite, "What's that like?"

"Pretty cool; we fished from thirty foot wooden trollers. There's about five hundred boats in the fleet and we were catching fish about fifteen hundred miles off the coast."

He had everyone's attention. "We towed two lines of fifty five gallon fuel drums behind the boat. As we ran out of fuel we'd bring in a full drum and fill our tank and then attach the empty drum to the string of empties. At night after fishing all day we'd all tie up together into one giant raft. With our lights on we looked like a floating city, all lit up in the middle of the Pacific. Caught a lot of fish, great times."

Too Tall took a swig of wine. "After this season, I was thinking of joining the Merchant Marine."

Ben piped up, "You can't do that Too Tall. Double Shot would lose his best friend."

Too Tall smiled and said with emphasis, "I jokes!"

After a thoughtful pause Marvin turned to Barry, "Where you going to fish tomorrow?" No secrets among friends. Barry savored the morsel he just swallowed then said, "Thought we'd head north to Sitka. Back to our old stomping grounds and fish the dogs off Hidden Falls (east side of Baranoff Island). Should be pretty good; how about you?"

"Probably down to Addington; chance there's gonna be some sockeye."

It went without saying that any information passed on at this table stayed at this table. Years of experience had taught them where to fish. And when any information was exchanged in public or over the radio, it was in code. The fleet had ears.

For example, Marvin might call Barry over the radio and say: "Lots of birds north of Noyes, over." Translation: plenty of fish south of Noyes Island.

Or Barry might call Marvin and say: "The dogs are showing up at the falls with plenty of clips."

Translation: lots of chum salmon returning to Hidden Falls hatchery. They both had their favorite spots.

Barry knew, without a doubt, that about this time of year chum salmon would be returning to the hatchery and even though they are a mid-value salmon, chances were he would catch enough to make a profit, maybe a big profit. There is money in volume.

On the other hand, a load of sockeye from Addington is at least twice as valuable as one of Chums, but it's a real gamble. Sometimes they are there, sometimes not. They're more difficult to find and catch than chums but the payoff can be big.

The table was silent as the crew digested the import of what was said. Crews never knew where they would be fishing until the skipper told them; usually at the last possible moment. Until then their lives were on hold. It was up to their skippers.

Barry looked over at David who was less interested in conversation and more focused on the meal. He asked, "Where's John?"

David poured another glassful of wine. "Not sure, said he had to meet up with a pal in the cannery; or something like that."

Although it was getting late, there was a couple more hours of daylight left. So while the others stayed aboard the Mary Ann, Sissy and I went ashore. We wandered together through the abandoned buildings. She was my tour guide.

As a young girl on her father's boat, Sissy had been here many times. For children of the fleet, the cannery at Steamboat Bay was a ready-made fantasy world; a great place to nurture a developing imagination. Now it was no more than a collection of empty warehouses. She said, "My grandfather worked here when he was a boy."

We went from building to building and room to room as she explained the canning process at Steamboat Bay. "This room is where they stored the cans. And this room is where the iron chinks were (machines that cleaned and prepared the fish for canning). This building is where the butchers worked. These are the retorts where they cooked the cans. This is where they sealed the cans. This is where they put on the labels. Those are the bunk houses where the workers lived." On and on she went.

I think at first she was a little nervous but by the time we entered the last building I had my arm around her shoulder and said, "Sissy relax. You're great. I hope you've been thinking of me because I've thought about you a lot." She looked up and smiled. I could feel her tenseness disappear. It had been a long time since I last held a woman.

"And this was our play room when the weather was bad." There were four lonely swings hanging from the rafters, sketches in crayon on the walls, a few pint-sized wooden tables and chairs, and just visible was a worn hopscotch pattern in the middle of the floor.

While I stood in square one, she walked over to a corner of the room. Standing tippy toe on a wooden crate she was able to reach behind the end rafter where it was nailed to the wall plate. And from a little cranny (a perfect hiding place), she pulled out a dusty old cigar box. Holding it in front of me she said with a smile, "I'd forgotten about this."

She opened her treasure box: A pink plastic barrette; two cockle shells; one small shiny garnet; a small piece of driftwood; a blue glass float; and a little ivory pendant on a fine gold chain. The ivory piece had yellowed with age but still visible on its surface was a scene of two finely etched (scrimshawed) dolphins leaping in aerobatic unison from rolling sea.

She held it out and said. "This belonged to my great great grandmother. I was just a little girl when my mother gave it to me. One day when Angie and me were here playing I put it in my treasure box for safe keeping. I thought I had lost it." She smiled, "but here it is." She slipped the pendant into her pocket and put the cigar box back into its hiding place. "Mom's gonna be happy."

We opened another door and were surprised by the watchman; a big burly mountain of a man at least six foot five with a huge scar running down the right side of his cheek from the tip of his ear lobe to the corner of his chin. I noticed his huge hands were covered with splotches of blue dye that glowed eerily under the dim florescent lighting.

He was Al Franco, one of the Franco brothers. It was his job to sell gas and ice and make sure the place didn't burn down. Standing just a foot or two in front of me he asked and demanded, with putrid breath, "what in the hell are you two doin in here? No one's allowed in this part of the cannery, understand!"

Then he noticed Sissy. His grin exposed rotting gums and gaps where teeth had fallen out. As he stood there he rubbed the right side of his face leaving a pigmented blue smear along his ugly scar. He stared long and hard at Sissy. It would have been bad for her had she been here alone.

She obviously felt uneasy around him.

I took her hand and she could feel me tense. I looked at him and said calmly, "Take it easy pal. We didn't know..."

But before I could finish my sentence the ape man screamed, "Stay out, ya understand! This here's private property!" He took a few steps backward and slammed the door in my face. I could still smell his breath. I turned to Sissy, "I guess that means the tour is over."

She turned to me and whispered, "Now that's a real asshole." Then she took hold of my shirt collar and pulled my mouth to hers and gave me a long warm kiss and said, "That's for being here with me."

And I replied, "You're welcome."

12

THE FRANCO BROTHERS

Al marched into the cannery office. The door slammed behind him. His older brother George, seated behind his desk and holding the phone to his ear looked up for a moment then turned back to the receiver and said, "Yes sir, Mr. Wang. We'll be ready."

Mr. Chin Wang was the president of Hong Kong Ltd. Import/Export. The cannery was just another subsidiary of that company. Its subsidiaries ranged from coal mines to casinos. His social circle was small and certainly didn't include the Franco brothers.

Al attempted to speak but his brother's raised finger immediately put a stop to that. George continued, "Yes sir, yes sir, I will sir." He paused then, "Good bye sir."

George hung up the receiver then asked, "What's up Al?"

Al stood at the window overlooking the dock and pointed down to the two figures illuminated by the security lights. "Those two, that's what."

"Isn't that the Thomas girl?" George asked.

"Yeah, cute little prissy Sissy, only she's not so little now. She's fishing with Barry Stahl and I think the guy's a deck hand on the Selkirk boat. I caught the two of them snooping around." He paused then added, "I'd like to have her to myself someday."

George perked up, "Did they see anything?"

Al stared out the window, ran his right thumb down the length of his scar and said, "I checked, and the door to the lab was left unlocked." He looked back at George and continued, "If they went into the west wing they probably got into our little lab and figured things out. It was that damn chink wannabe scientist's fault."

George who had little patience for incompetence and excuses, yelled: "You're the damn watchman. You should've made sure the door was locked."

Without thinking Al blurted out, "I should have killed him sooner. He was always a problem."

"You killed Lee Wang, our chemist, when?"

Al started to stutter, "This afternoon. I was meaning to tell you. He got greedy and sold five grams of coke to that recruit, John Geeser. The little shit's been rippin us off."

Al looked down at his stained hands. "Don't worry, I cut him up and stuffed his body in one of them fifty five gallon drums out back and filled it with that Super Blue lye; spilled some of the dust on me while I was mixing it up. The stuff's gonna have to wear off. In a couple of weeks there's gonna be nothing left of that little bastard."

George thought for a moment then said loud and clear, "You dumb shit, that little lab rat was the son of Chin Wang, our boss! Understand? Chin Wang is mister China Mafia, got it!"

Al Franco, a stupid ox of a man who really didn't care what his brother was trying to say, but just to appease him said, "Yeah, got it." And then added, "So what are we gonna do?"

George said, "Well if we don't figure something out we're both gonna die and it won't be painless." He opened a desk drawer and pulled out his 45 auto and set it down next to the phone and stared hard at Al.

That got Al's attention. At heart he was really just a bully. He stuttered, "I'm sorry George." George after a thoughtful pause put the gun back into the drawer. "Okay, okay, what about this; John Geeser is fishing on the Harvester, right?"

Al answered, "Yeah that's right, along with Sissy and her sister."

George began to form a plan. "Okay here's what we do. First I tell mister Wang that his boy was murdered by Geeser for a little coke."

Al grumbled, "Yeah, what next?"

George continued, "We let him decide what he wants done, and he'll probably say kill Geeser. That's what you're gonna do and that'll get us off the hook. Come to think of it, we'll probably even get a reward. We might even move up in the organization. You'll get to spend some quality time with Sissy."

"You're a genius George."

13

A TIME TO GO FISHING

Morning came much, much too soon. The vibration of our idling engine along with noises from the surrounding fleet signaled the start of the season. There was excitement in the air.

Ben poked his face down through the hatch, "Up and at um' Dylan. We're goin' fishing."

Too Tall was at the stove and the rest of the crew were at the table. I took my place and thought about Sissy and how fortunate I was to be here. Breakfast was especially good.

"I'm going to miss you," were the last words I shouted from deck as we passed the Harvester and headed out to sea. A little too shy to shout back, Sissy just smiled and mouthed the words, "Me too."

All night long outside the bay the wind had been blowing at fifty knots plus, but in our sanctuary all was dead calm. Not even a breeze.

By morning, the storm had blown itself out and the water was glassy smooth again. In dense fog we cruised out of the bay past Point Incarnation and headed west.

Not too long afterwards we rounded Cape Ulitka and turned south for Cape Addington, that rugged promontory off the southwest end of Noyes Island. It is a place known by sea lions and fisherman alike as one of the premier fishing grounds of all southeast Alaska.

14

TO CATCH A SALMON

Marvin was at the wheel and with our seine skiff in tow we cruised southward along Noyes Island's west coast on the hunt for fish. Fortunately for us the weather was perfect. But on stormy days this unprotected rocky coastline is exposed to the full fury of the sea. Here, mother nature rules.

He knew the signs by heart. Depth, bottom type, water temperature, presence of bait fish, birds, water current, gut feeling, etc. They are all clues.

As we approached Shaft Rock (that huge granite monolith that rises straight up from the sea to a hundred feet or more) Marvin eased off on the throttle and put the gear into neutral as we attached one end of the seine to the skiff.

The drill is straightforward. Based on years of experience the skipper finds the spot where he knows fish should be. In essence, salmon migrate in cold deep water following huge schools of bait fish (e.g. herring). Once their prey is found, the salmon begin to feed. The bait panic and try to escape into shallower water. Soon it is a scene of utter frenzy that attracts more fish and more and more sea birds; which attracts Marvin.

The back deck is reserved for the net and its working lines. Here the heavy seine net is stacked in the center of the deck in a particular way (for sure no easy task), and on either side of it and in similar manner are stacked the lead line (weights), and cork line (floats). Once the net is pulled into the water by the seine skiff, the lead line sinks the bottom edge of the net while the cork line keeps the top edge afloat.

Double Shot is the skiff man on the Mary Ann. He is the best in the fleet. When seiners are fishing (in close quarters) on the same school of salmon, it is the skiff man's skill, experience, and aggressiveness that spells success or failure. On command from the skipper and at full power he will drag the net, float line, and lead line off the seiner to make a net barrier twelve hundred feet long and forty feet deep in front of the migrating salmon. And in no time at all that huge pile of net will disappear off the back deck. Words of caution: "stand clear."

With the seine skiff's throttle at full and rpm's screaming just shy of red line, the net is held taught and straight against the current.

At first the salmon aren't visible but the skipper knows they are there. Soon a fish jumps clear of the surface; then another and another. Before long, the school has moved up against the net barrier. Experience tells the skipper to wait, wait, and wait until he feels the time is right to bring in the net. If he waits too long, the crowded salmon will either dive under the net or back off and head around. If he doesn't wait long enough the fish haven't arrived. Either way, an empty net (water haul) is all that will be brought aboard.

At just the right moment (gut feeling), before the fish escape, Marvin will order Double Shot to make his giant "U" turn around the salmon and head back to the boat. In this way, the salmon are encircled and the net is set. Once the skiff makes it back to the boat, the tow line is hooked to the power block, hanging from the boom, which then begins to haul in the net, lead line, and cork line; another well-choreographed dance. The power skiff is then freed from the net and harnessed to the opposite side of the seiner. This time at full reverse throttle, the skiff maintains a constant pull to keep the seiner from becoming tangled in the net or even capsizing (which could easily happen without the skiff's assistance). A net full of hundreds of tons of fish that decide to dive has flipped seine boats even in the calmest sea.

Just prior to winching in the net, the purse line, which runs free through a series of rings attached to the lead line, is pulled tight. This effectively cinches the net into a bag of salmon. The net is steadily brought out of the water as it is pulled through the power block. And the fish are concentrated more and more into a tight mass in the section of the net that remains in the water. From there, the fish are brailed by hand (dip netted) into the hold, until the power block can lift the heavily loaded net and pour its contents also into the hold.

I should mention that after the power block has pulled the net out of the water, the net has to be re-run through the block and re-piled on the back deck and ready for the next set. A routine repeated fifteen to twenty times a day; "water hauls" are not appreciated. Working under the power block suspended from the boom ten feet or so above the deck, the crewmen (and crew women) work feverishly to stack the net and gear. The longer the net is out of the water, fewer fish are caught. Of course, as the net comes through the block, so do any snagged salmon (with their jaws wrapped in the web) and all the planktonic critters that are entangled during the set.

To free a snagged salmon from the net by hand is an unpleasant task which unavoidably results in cuts and punctures. To make matters worse, by the force of gravity, many of the hitchhikers detach from the web to rain down on the crew. These are mainly jellyfish.

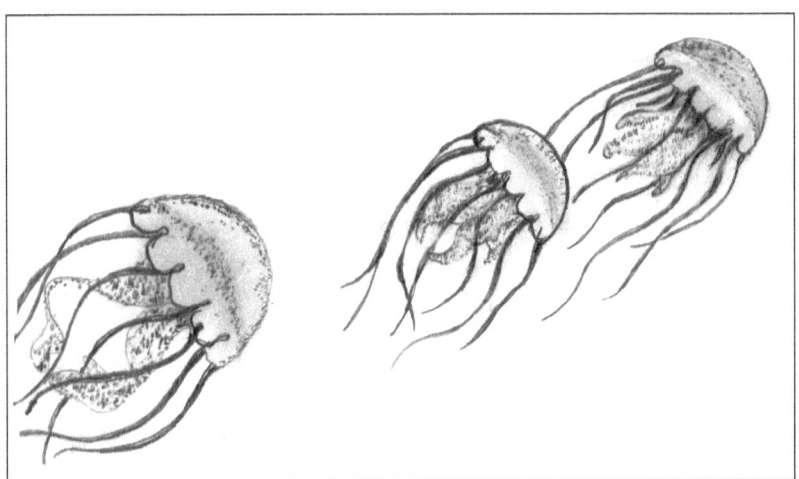

They've been around for millions of years and there are billions of them. They are Mother Nature's planktonic parachutes that drift aimlessly with the prevailing oceanic currents. As these predators glide through the water no one can deny their beauty and grace. They are an absence of resistance. Bodies composed of a jelly-like substance from which their name is derived, they may range in size from a fraction of an inch to six feet plus in diameter; translucent or of many colors.

But most importantly, from the perspective of the crew, is the lacy ribbon like tissue which hangs from the underside of their gelatinous discs; beauty and danger; form and function. The delicate tissue is laden with thousands of venomous stinging cells (nematocysts) that paralyze prey which is then consumed by the carnivorous jellyfish. Woe to the crewman whose bare skin contacts a jellyfish. The words "burning grief," come to mind.

Crewmen who pile web under the power block always wear rain gear even on the hottest of days, for they will be rained down upon by showers of goo.

15

A RECRUIT'S PERSPECTIVE

There were no other boats around and by mid-morning the fog had burned off. We were alone off Shaft Rock and sockeye were all around us and Marvin's personality changed from mild mannered to slave driver (did I say he mellowed with age?).

Ben, Too Tall, and me stood on the back deck stacking the gear as it was pulled aboard. Trying to stack the net in a neat pile as it falls from the power block is a job I won't soon forget. On my left was Ben stacking corks and Too Tall to my right stacking lead line and rings. Finally the net was stacked in a neat pile and Double Shot began another run.

At first all was calm; only a few salmon could be seen swimming within the huge enclosure of the pursed net. As more net was brought aboard and the enclosure became smaller, more and more sockeye became visible, and the crew's excitement began to build (there was even a smile on Double Shot's face). As the process continued and the salmon were crowded to the Mary Ann's starboard side, the water became a roiling mass of fins and bodies.

Too Tall grabbed the long handled plunger (looks like a toilet bowl plunger), and forced it up and down into the water which scared fish from escaping through gaps in the net next to the hull. It was an amazing sight. Finally, as the last of the net (money bag) was lifted aboard, the weight of it all caused the fifty five foot Mary Ann to list to the point that her starboard gunnel was almost underwater. The boom, shackles, lines, and hoist were all strained to their breaking point. At which time thousands of salmon were then spilled on deck and into the hold. In an instant the status quo was restored and the adrenaline rush was over.

Ben turned to me and said, "A few years ago we were hauling in a bag of dogs and a brand new block snapped; too much weight. It flew through the air like a rocket and hit one of the crew in the back of the head; killed him instantly. Turned out the block was defective."

Our forty ton hold was half filled from that first set. As the last of the fish that had spilled onto the deck were pitched into the hold, Marvin said, "Couple more sets like that boys and we'll be plugged (hold full of fish)."

No time to rest; time to get ready for another set. I just followed orders: hurry up, pick up those fish; hurry up, get the skiff hooked up; hurry up, tie off that line; hurry up; hurry up. Everything was hurry up. Then Marvin brought the Mary Ann back into position and Double Shot was on his way towing the net for another set.

Ben slapped me on the shoulder. "Time to relax Dylan let's eat."

Off came my rain gear. That was a happy crew that sat at the galley's table. Too Tall's grilled cheese sandwiches (Cheddar) were exceptionally tasty.

Lucky or not, for the rest of the day we kept catching fish. At five o'clock, the first opening of the season was ended and we with our hold filled to the hatch cover with prime sockeye were headed back to Klawock.

Later that evening after a roast beef dinner, I sat on the net pile with a cup of Too Tall's coffee enjoying the gentle roll of the ocean as the sinking sun filled the western sky with a golden glow and brilliant streaks of violet; announcing the end of a perfect day. I found my place and I was hooked.

We passed a pod of Humpback Whales lazily migrating north to their summer feeding grounds in the Bering Sea; huge creatures almost as large as the Mary Ann. Reminders of days gone by.

16

LEVIATHANS

Without a doubt, whaling was grueling and dangerous work. Voyages lasted up to five years or more and then after returning home whalemen could easily spend their entire earnings in less than a month. And then it was back to sea they went.

For the most part it was just boring work. Days and months were spent searching for their quarry. Sailors longed for home. Then the call, "Thar she blows," would come from above and in an instant the monotony was gone.

Off in the distance, the crew would catch a brief glimpse of a dark form breaking the surface. Just long enough for it to exhale a warm moist alveolar mist; proof of the prize.

The scene aboard the ship was controlled chaos. Silently the ship made its way close, but not too close. The captain's order: "Heave to," and the ship was brought into the wind and to a stop. His next order, "Whaleboats, down and away," and five oarsmen, a helmsman, and a harpooner were off to the hunt.

From the deep darkness, the exhausted whale came to the surface to rest. Stealth; silently, the whaleboat crept close behind the great leviathan's head. The harpooner ready at the bow and at exactly the right moment, he plunged his irons deep into the whale's vitals.

A hundred tons of perfection that had lived at peace for over fifty years is then in an instant panic stricken plunging to the deep. The air breathing mammal descended three, four, five thousand feet below; all the while tethered to the little dory waiting on the surface; waiting, waiting, waiting. Then, in the next moment the scene was pure adrenaline as the whaleboat and its crew is pulled at break-neck speed through the sea by the unseen goliath below (a Nantuckett sleigh ride).

And then no longer able to hold his breath, the whale slowly turned upward, back toward the surface. The harpoon line went slack. The whaleboat came to a stop and the sea calmed. Not a ripple. Then, all at once in a great display of foam and spray, an explosive breeching shattered the stillness as the whale broke the surface. A red vapor cloud betrayed his mortal wound and he became still. The drama may have been repeated again and again depending on the skill of the harpooner and the size and spirit of the whale. But in the end the dead whale was towed back to the ship to be butchered and its blubber rendered into golden brown oil, three hundred barrels from a large whale plus its baleen. And from the bulbous head of the coveted Sperm Whale, an additional fifty barrels of the most valuable oil of all, Spermaceti.

Vincent St. James was born and raised in New Bedford, Massachusetts. His father was a whaleman as was his grandfather as were all the men of the St. James family. They lived and died whalemen. So, in 1829 at the age of fifteen Vincent signed on as a deck hand aboard the whaling schooner Southern Cross out of New Bedford.

During that first voyage, Vincent made friends with the ship's carpenter Jules Sorenson.

In 1810, when Jules was not much more that a boy he made up his mind to escape a life of poverty in Sundvall, Sweden and indentured himself to the

Russian American Company at New Archaengel (Sitka, Alaska) for a period of seven years. Unfortunately those grand promises of opportunity never material-ized. Jules had traded the drudgery of a cod fisherman at home for worse: the drudgery of saltery laborer under one cruel Russian taskmaster after another. All were bent on breaking his spirit.

After three years, Jules escaped from that Russian outpost as a stowaway on an American freighter bound for San Francisco where he signed onto an American whaler as a deckhand.

Jules took to whaling and eventually became a well-respected harpooner among the whalemen of New Bedford. The two crossed harpoons tattooed across his back were proof of his prowess. Maybe he was tired of killing whales or maybe just bored. Whatever the reason though, after twenty years, his job became rou-tine and he became careless.

One uneventful day while Jules was busy on deck splicing lines and repair-ing worn gear Vincent sat down beside him asked the about his days as a har-pooner and how he had come to lose his leg.

The harpooner gazed at his young friend, remembering himself years ear-lier, eager to be a great whaleman. He said, "Ya shore my friend, we were off da Azores and Da hunt been goot tat day; ve ban surrounded by many vales." He paused as he rubbed his knee, "Ya, I remember dat well. Da beast lay asleep on da surface and da helmsman brought us close by. It was a perfect strike. My iron went deep and true and da vale burst alive and sounded. By da time he came to rest deep down, maybe five hundred fathoms of line payed out of our casks. For hours ve sat and waited and by da time he came back up, another four of our boats came to da hunt."

Then Jules became silent. He stood up, took hold of the rail and stared out at the horizon. He reached back into his memory, "Another harpoon another strike. Each time he came to da surface a red cloud hung over us. He was a large bull and would give twenty five casks of sperm oil, or more. He dragged our boat for miles. Finally da beast came to the surface and became still. We waited as always and he never moved. We came alongside and as I raised my lance to finish him off, he came alive, and in his final flurry I bin knocked to da bottom of da boat. I remember da feel of da cold steel blade. No pain, no, no, just a heavy quick slice. When I woke he lie dead but my harpoon days were over."

Jules was too valuable a hand to lose so the captain assigned him to be ship's carpenter.

Jules place his hand on Vincent's shoulder. "That was a long time ago," he paused, "be careful and always expect da worse and you might survive."

Then, toward the end of that voyage off the southern coast of Greenland, one night during a winter storm, Jules was swept overboard. A rolling pitching deck is no place for a one legged man. No one saw him go overboard. He just disappeared.

The next morning, Captain Milsap led the crew in a short prayer. After a tearless eulogy the men were dismissed. Vincent stood by the rail staring down at the sea, mourning the loss of his friend and mentor. Captain Milsap stood beside him and said, "Mr. Saint James, from now on you're the ship's carpenter, congratulation."

As the ship's carpenter/cooper, Vincent made emergency repairs and built barrels; lots and lots of barrels. And of course he took his turn in the whaleboats. All able bodied seamen took their turn.

That first voyage was a success: five hundred barrels of whale oil and more than a thousand barrels of spermaceti. After three years and two months at sea and two hundred dollars in his pocket, he considered himself a whaleman. To honor his old friend Jules, Vincent had a pair of crossed harpoons tattooed across his forearm.

After just two months at home and his pay spent, Vincent signed on as ship's carpenter for the bark (barque) Dora. With a two hundred ton displacement and capacity for eighteen hundred barrels she was considerably larger and faster than the Southern Cross. Among whalemen the Dora was known as a "greasy" ship which meant she brought back a lot of oil.

The year was 1846 and it was Vincent's third voyage on the Dora. They were four months out of New Bedford and two thousand miles west of Chile in the South Pacific. It was December and for two months they had been hunting Sperm Whales on their winter breeding grounds. They had four hundred barrels of sperm oil, a thousand barrels of whale oil, and nearly five thousand pounds of baleen aboard. The crew was confident that at the rate things were going, they'd be returning home by spring. Funny thing about sailors: when in port they talk about how much they miss the sea. And when at sea it's how much they miss home.

The captain's log read: "December 24, 1846; A calm sea; another large pod of whales. The whale boats had been lowered and were away. Soon after, the first cow was taken and was being towed back to the ship. The oarsmen were having a tough go of it beating back to windward. A large bull was also struck with four whaleboats in pursuit. After more than an hour he broke loose of the harpoons and in his fury turned on the Dora."

The Dora shuddered as the great giant rammed her side. Again and again until finally, with her port side "stove in," the ship began to sink. Slowly but surely and nothing could be done to save her. Provisions and supplies were quickly salvaged. The forty one whalemen and their captain in six whaleboats watched as their ship sank while the two dead whales remained on the surface in a sheen of red.

Captain Potts set their course for nearby Henderson Island (about five hundred miles east northeast of Pitcairn Island) and within the week they made landfall. The little island is no more than just thirty square miles of raised coral reef with a crown of dense jungle. Other than shellfish, birds, and their eggs there was no other game, and little fresh water.

After two weeks on the island and with their supplies running dangerously low, captain Potts was convinced that to remain on the island was not an option. He thought that under sail and with the prevailing easterly they could make the eighteen hundred mile trip to Tahiti within a month. But Vincent and four of the whalemen thought differently and decided to stay put. Without objection the captain accepted their decision. He knew fewer men in the boats meant rations lasting longer.

So after shaking Vincent's hand as well as the other four, the captain stepped into the waiting whaleboat and bid them, "Stay strong lads and may the lord grant us all protection." That said, his boat was pushed away.

Vincent felt a twinge of abandonment as he stood with his mates and watched the six whaleboats return back to the sea through the churning surf. The boats became smaller and smaller to be no more than just dots on the horizon and finally altogether gone. And Vincent and his four crew mates were left with a one week supply of hard tack and salt pork.

Captain Potts set their course west north west. Not very accurate by modem standards but Theodore Potts was at home on the sea, and having been in similar situations before reasoned that as long as their rations held out they would survive to be rescued. Tahiti or any other Polynesian island would do. Whichever, it didn't matter. And Potts was a good navigator.

At twenty three degrees latitude, Captain Potts and his crew were just north of the Tropic of Capricorn. Here the trade winds blow predominantly from the northeast towards the southwest. Unfortunately for them, the prevailing ocean current coupled with the wind had pushed them further south than Potts calculated and the sum effect was their eighteen hundred mile trip to Tahiti turned into a grueling thirty five hundred mile voyage to Pago Pago.

It rained once and they captured what little rainwater they could. Their provisions lasted three weeks and by the end of the fifth week the men began to die of starvation.

At first the dead were buried at sea. According to tradition they were sewn into their clothing and after a short prayer committing their bodies to the deep, they were passed over the side. Time moved at a snail's pace. No rescue. The crew was in a very bad way.

Then as more time passed and by majority vote for the sake of survival it was decided that they would eat the dead. Those were terrible days.

The last poor fellow to be eaten was cabin boy Albert Potts; Theodore's youngest nephew. The fifteen year old boy always wanted to be just like his guardian uncle. Yes it was a terrible time but by the end of the ninth week, the captain and twenty six of his crew survived to be rescued.

And three and a half months later when captain Potts and the rescue party returned to Henderson Island they found Vincent and his four shipmates alive and well and in the company of friendly Polynesian "savages."

Once they were told of their shipmate's fate, their initial state of elation turned to grief.

After returning home to New Bedford, Vincent swore he would never again put out to sea, at least not voluntarily.

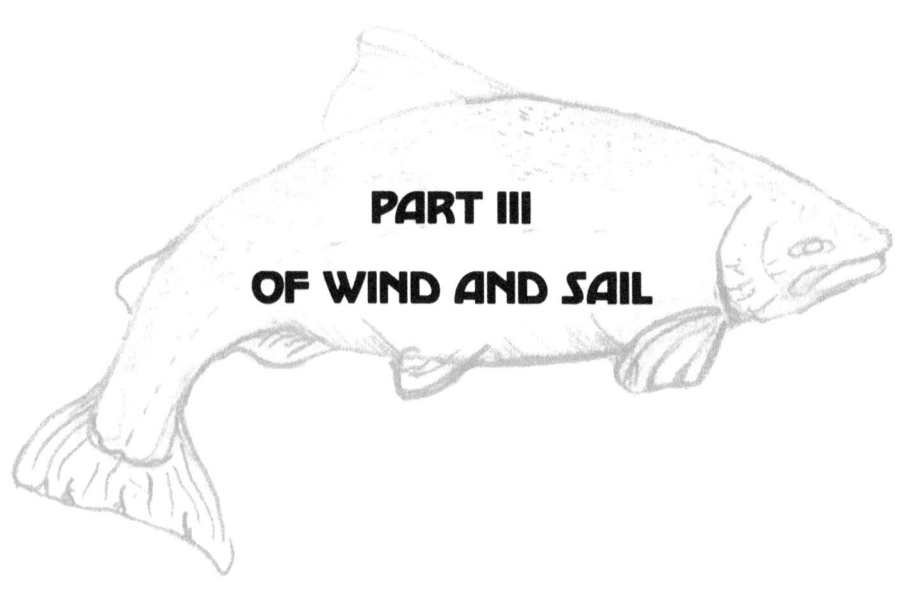

PART III
OF WIND AND SAIL

17

SHANGHAIED

Safe at home; it was a comfortable feeling at least for a while. Vincent decided he had enough of whaling and was determined to fit into a life on land. And New Bedford, that beehive of boat building, was an excellent fit for a man like him. With his experience he became a carpenter at McKay's Shipyard. By day he immersed himself in his work and by night he could be found at The Oak Tiller (a local tavern and favorite watering hole for shipwrights).

Try as he may though, and no matter how much he drank, he could not forget the Dora and his lost shipmates. To make matters worse, the story of his survival and the fate of the Dora became legend. Fame made Vincent uneasy and he set his mind to become an average "landlubber." Fortunately, time marched on and the popularity of his past began to fade.

Content and bored. Vincent still enjoyed his job but like his life, it too became routine. One morning while caulking the barque Terra, for its maiden voyage as a whaler in the south Atlantic, a support beam snapped. Vincent and two others were trapped underneath the hull. While he lay there on the ground, flat as a sand dollar with his face pressed hard against the Cypress planking, Vincent remembered the advice of his friend Jules: "Be careful and always expect the worse and you might survive."

It took most of the day to free them. Afterwards he thought how ironic after surviving eighteen years at sea and now to have almost have died on dry land in this shipyard under a whaler.

That night he paid a visit to the Oak Tiller. It was late, his friends had all gone home and Vincent sat by himself. The place was almost deserted except for George, the bartender, and the two men at a back table who had the look of seasoned whalemen: dark; rugged; and a touch of wildness beneath a thin veneer of civilization and grease. He finished his drink and was about to leave when the tavern keeper poured him "another" and said, "From those fellows Vincent," and nodded in the direction of the two whalemen. Vincent turned to their direction and raised his glass. They motioned him over and he obliged.

He sat down and the somewhat familiar larger man, asked in deep baritone, "How ya been matey?"

The lantern's light was dim, too dim for detail, but he'd recognize that voice anywhere. It belonged to the Irishman, Conan O'Riley (first mate on the Dora and a survivor from one of the whaleboats). Vincent's life had come full circle.

Two minutes into their conversation and the years just slipped away. At first it was just small talk. Conan introduced his companion, "This here is Gabriel." The small swarthy man put out his hand and with a strong Hispanic accent, "I am Gabriel Lasotta. Mister Saint James I have heard many stories of your survival on Henderson Island. You..."

Vincent stopped him in mid-sentence. "The real story lies with those in the whaleboats."

Lasotta raised a finger, "Yes that may be true sir, but you saved your men and more important you saved their souls."

Conan added, "Aye Vincent, those men you saved can sleep soundly, as they did not eat their shipmates."

Vincent took another drink and quietly reflected on what was just said. Conan broke the silence, "Bowheads, Vincent; Bowheads."

Vincent hadn't a clue what his friend was talking about.

Conan continued, "The old grounds are used up. No more whales; Atlantic, Pacific, Tropics; all gone. But Vincent there's a new beast, the Bowhead, and he lives in the Arctic."

After two hundred plus years of whaling pressure in the Atlantic and Pacific, the great stocks including the Blue, Humpback, Gray, Right, and Sperm had all but disappeared. Whalers had pursued the pods almost to extinction further and further south into the Antarctic around Cape Horn through the tropics and north up the coast of the Americas.

The final performance of the saga would be would be staged in the Bering, Chukchi, and Arctic Seas; the last foothold of the great leviathans.

Conan placed his hand on Vincent's shoulder. "Matey, he is a monster. He'll deliver four hundred barrels of oil and five hundred pounds of baleen. Aye lad, he is the future and we seek his audience. Our ship is the Thomas B and her master is Samuel Milsap. A fine vessel and a fine master."

The Thomas B was a three-masted whaling bark built in New Bedford, Massachusetts in 1834. With a displacement of 305 tons and carrying a crew of 41 she was one of the largest whalers of her day and capable of long extended voyages. From the day she had been launched Benjamin Milsap, of Southern Cross fame, had been her master. He was the driving force that would push her through the Bering Sea into the Arctic. Vincent knew captain Milsap as fine and single minded as any master, anywhere. Vincent also knew the ship. She had been built at McKays and was there the previous year for routine maintenance.

In those days, whalers had a mix of crews: those who volunteered and those who were shanghaied.

Conan said, "Matey, we're in need of another whaleman."

Vincent felt the tone of their conversation change. "Is that why you're here?" And Conan replied, "Pleasure and business, matey; pleasure and business. The pleasure is meeting up with you again and the business is the offer of adventure. The tide is high at four o'clock this morning and we'll be shoving off then." Vincent paused, "Conan, my friend, I appreciate the offer but have a new life now. I'm done with whaling. Life's good here in New Bedford. So I have to decline but wish you good luck."

Conan turned to Gabriel just long enough for a wink and a nod. He turned back to Vincent. "Well then matey, sorry you feel that way. We have a tide to catch."

Conan said, "Next time we're back we'll be sure to look you up." Then, "Are ya sure you won't be joinin' us?"

Vincent remained steady, "Sorry boys my place is here."

The sound of two chairs scraping across the hardwood floor echoed across the tavern as the two whalemen rose.

Vincent shook their hands and watched as they walked out the door into the night, then whispered to himself, "Good luck mates." It was late.

Home wasn't that far away. Just two blocks down the cobblestone walkway, across the street, turn right, then two more blocks to The Inn of the Little Blue Heron, the only boarding house on the waterfront. Susan, the proprietress always left a plate of bread pudding and a candle burning in the window to light the way.

About half way home he heard footsteps approach from behind. He was about to turn when suddenly something hard came down on the back of his head. Then it was just darkness.

Later that morning he awoke on a bunk in the forecastle of the Thomas B. Still a little dazed, he looked up to see Conan standing over him saying, "Sorry matey, I had to do it. Captains orders and all that, ya understand."

Vincent's first reaction was anger. Then just as quickly, that melted away like a load off his shoulders. Conan looked down at his friend. "Matey, you're a whaleman. Maybe someday you'll be a landlubber but not now. Maybe not never."

With that his friend climbed up the ladder to the foredeck.

Vincent followed. The roll of the ocean felt good. The smell of the sea was nothing like that of New Bedford. It was a clean fresh smell; and overhead, the sounds of a thousand chattering sea gulls. He felt as if he had come home as he watched the shores of Nantucket Island gradually disappear behind the Thomas B's stern. Nothing ahead but open ocean.

18

DEVILS REEF

It was the first week of February 1849 and the Thomas B found herself in the midst of a blizzard. Twelve hours and thirty miles earlier under a clear crisp sky and on a calm sea they had left sight of Prince Rupert. By nightfall they were fighting to stay alive twenty miles out in the middle of Dixon Entrance, that wild stretch of deep open-ocean separating British Columbia from Alaska's Alexander Archipelego.

It was an especially very bad place to be at this time of the year.

Early on, the first mate begged captain Milsap to turn south back to Prince Rupert, all to no avail. The skipper stood his ground and stayed the course, north.

The swells became mountain ranges and the Thomas B grew smaller as the storm continued to grow. Hurricane force winds blew the tops off the monstrous waves into which the helmsman fought to keep their bow pointed. No time to panic. All hands were on deck securing hatches, and up in the rigging reefing in the sails, and tying down anything that might be swept overboard.

Their tasks completed, the captain screamed to be heard, just barely, above the roar of the tempest. "Well boys that's all we can do. Whatever happens to us now is out of our hands." He ordered all hands below to wait out the storm. The first mate lashed himself to the wheel.

Vincent braced himself against the bulkhead and his bunk. The swinging lantern that hung from the overhead, cast a flickering dim light on the terrified faces of his shipmates. When the hatch blew open, the light was extinguished and all became dark. The roaring wind that blew through the rigging sounded as if it came straight out of hell, demonic.

Gabriel's voice called out of the darkness, "Lord, please Lord save us. Oh my God please don't let us die. Not like this!" Conan put his hand on Vincent's shoulder and said, "Well Vincent lad, looks like I got ya into a real mess."

Vincent calmly replied, "Don't fuss about it. It's just fate." To which Conan replied, "Just the same matey, I'm sorry." Gabriel spoke, "Mister Saint Clair are we going to survive?"

Vincent could hear the terror in the young man's voice. He lied, "don't worry, I've been through a lot worse in my time."

Every seaman knows about fate and some come to prefer the deep as their final resting place rather than in the ground. As it was said, "Who wouldn't prefer to be consumed by the fish rather than by the worms."

In darkness the tempest raged on and on. The wind switched directly out of the west and had driven them well off course. If their luck held, it might just have brought them to the safety of Cordova Bay.

Had it not been for Devils Reef.

In an instant the port bow was crushed. It was simply terrible. First the impact of the collision followed by the flood of the ocean pouring through the splintered maw into the pitch blackness of the crowded forecastle and then the primal screams of men and boys trapped to be drowned; nowhere to go. It was out of their hands. Prayers directed to their God begging for mercy. And finally, their cries were silenced.

19

SURVIVAL

At the south end of Dall Island is the rocky shoreline of Cape Muzon (fifty four degrees thirty nine minutes north longitude and one hundred thirty two degrees forty minutes west latitude). A heavily forested low mountain range borders the beach.

It was a golden sunrise and here among the other remnants of the Thomas B, Vincent awoke. He was alone and strewn along the tide flats for miles were the huge copper rendering pots, barrels, pieces of decking, a hand axe, rigging, bricks from the tryworks, tools, sailcloth, sealed crates, and a variety of other miscellaneous items.

He remembered grabbing onto the carpenters tool box and then being swept out of the forecastle and into the sea. Now, there at his feet was the large wooden box that kept him afloat.

Snow covered the forest and he was soaking wet and cold. He knew somehow he must build a fire or die right here on this foreign shore.

Maybe as some believe, there is no such thing as fate. I think not. For within that carpenters box was a piece of fine grained quartz; just a rock. But when struck against steel it produced sparks.

He shivered. The morning was crisp and peaceful except for the call of a passing shorebird. With the sea at his back, he made his way up the beach to a shallow cave at the foot of the mountain. Strewn about its entrance were numerous fallen and centuries old, moss covered cedars; casualties of past winter storms and shallow soils.

From one of the old cedars he stripped off lengths of tinder dry bark and patches of grey moss (known by the natives as "old man's beard"). A few strikes of the flint across the side of his axe produced a tiny smoldering ember. His very breath nurtured this ember into a tiny flame. Moss, bark, twigs, more bark, drift wood, and then fire. There's something about such a fire. As it warmed his body it strengthened his spirit.

He spent the rest of the day collecting Thomas B debris off the beach. In one crate labeled CAPTAIN MILSAP PRIVATE, he found a variety of dry items including clothing, books, a bottle of rum, tins of smoked oysters, a pipe and tobacco, and at the bottom of the crate and wrapped in oil cloth was Captain Milsap's forty four caliber Sharps rifle and ammunition.

There was no moon that night and a cold north wind blew but sitting by the fire and wearing a dry pair of the captain's britches, he was confident he would survive.

He could hear the sound of the surf breaking on the beach below. A swoosh followed by a long relaxed stillness, another swoosh, and so on. It was a familiar soothing sound.

Totally exhausted, he barely managed another swig of rum. The liquid felt warm as it passed down his throat. He threw more wood onto the fire then lay down on a mattress of fragrant cedar boughs. And with a piece of sailcloth over him he fell into a fitful sleep. He dreamed of that last night aboard the Thomas B, his shipmates, New Bedford, and Jules Sorensen. He thought somehow though he would survive.

The next morning he awoke to an excited commotion in the trees above. He lay still and through one open eye watched as a gang of boisterous ravens crowded the lower tree limbs directly over his head. It was obvious he was the center of their attention which brought to mind the carcass of a beached whale he once observed. It was a feast served up by Mother Nature for the multitude of wildlife which gorged itself on the decaying flesh.

Fully rested, he stood, stretched, and faced his company. "So what's the hubbub?"

Without so much as a chirp the startled visitors took wing and disappeared into the forest. He whispered after them, "Sorry boys, but I'm still alive."

All that remained of his fire were a few glowing embers and as he bent down to add more wood he spotted movement on the beach.

There were nine natives scavenging through the debris scattered across the beach. They appeared to be prisoners of four larger individuals armed with clubs. One who barked out orders carried a musket and was obviously in command. The prisoners carried their finds on cedar bark litters and in large woven baskets.

One who Vincent estimated to be not more than five feet tall, smaller than the rest, couldn't keep up with the others. After one of the guards screamed at him, he hesitated for just a moment and was immediately thrown to the ground and then savagely beaten. The unfortunate fellow lay flat on his back . The other prisoners appeared terrified. One who reached out to his fallen comrade was beaten and pushed away. Finally the guard with the musket pointed it at the un-moving body and pulled the trigger.

It wouldn't fire; probably a wet flint. So he just kicked the lifeless body a few more times, turned to the other guards, barked a few more orders and the prisoners were forced to continue on with their labor, leaving the poor fellow behind.

Eventually they picked up every bit of debris they thought of value. Then the head man cast one last look across the beach and satisfied there was noth-ing else worth taking, he ordered everyone into their canoes. Moments later the canoes disappeared into the distance leaving the lonely body behind.

Vincent made his way down the beach to the motionless figure. At first he thought the little man was dead. He had been left to die and most certainly would have. As Vincent stood there staring down at the castaway and not knowing what to do, the little man opened his eyes.

The sun's blinding glare caused Vincent's face to be lost in darkness. So the little man, frightened and in pain, had no idea of who Vincent was or what he was going to do.

The shadow disappeared as Vincent bent down. He spoke slow and calm, "Are you all right?"

No response. "Don't worry, I won't hurt you." No response.

Vincent pointed to himself, "Vincent, my name is Vincent."

It became clear that Vincent wanted to help. The little man spoke softly, "Ven sant?"

20

MOI-YO EMYA KLOO

Vincent put an arm around the little man's shoulder and helped him sit up. He looked at Vincent and managed to say, "Moi-yo emya Kloo," and again, "Moi-yo emya Kloo." Vincent nodded and smiled.

It must have been fate. Vincent remembered the first time he heard Jules Sorensen speak Russian to one of the crew on the Southern Cross. Vincent was fascinated by all that jibber jabber, so with time to spare and thanks to Jules and the Russian harpooner, Vincent became bilingual at a most rudimentary level.

At that time in history, fur trade (mainly sea otter) between the Russian empire and the natives of coastal Alaska was well established. So the little fellow thought Vincent must have been another Russian trader. He had said, "My name is Kloo."

Vincent thought, "Thank you Jules," then gently took hold of Kloo's hand and said, "Ya Drewg (I am a friend)."

Kloo nodded and smiled.

A bond of friendship, with survival in common, was established between the two men.

Vincent carried Kloo back to the cave and placed him on his sleeping platform. A sip or two of captain Milsap's rum and the little man was re-energized. Again in Russian, Kloo said, "I am Tlingit from the village of Klawock."

Vincent smiled. "And I am American from the village of New Bedford, America; not Russian."

That drew a blank stare. So Vincent asked, "Who were they and why did they hurt you?" Kloo spoke one word, "Haida," then he lay back on the platform and closed his eyes. Vincent turned his attention to the business of reviving the fire.

With the passage of time, Kloo's wounds healed. He was a good student and learned to speak English. Vincent was impressed by his friend's ability.

If Vincent was ever to return to civilization he felt Kloo was his ticket. With the threat of the Haida returning, their plan was to remain hidden during the day and forage at night. Kloo was Vincent's survival guide and teacher. And so, what at first appeared as just a barren shore, turned into a veritable cornucopia. Clams, abalone, sea cucumbers, octopus, fish, limpets, and a host of other creatures which escape description were there for the taking and became tasty ingredients in Kloo's soups. Just about anything that moved went into the pot.

To keep their fires secret, they were built at the rear of the cave so that the smoke disappeared up through the cracks in the ceiling to dissipate into the mossy forest floor above leaving no telltale sign for anyone to discover.

One day Vincent remarked, "You speak Russian very well."

Without looking up Kloo continued stirring the pot. He tasted his brew and after a savoring moment he began, "My father was a fur trader from up north. His name was Yakovitch; a Russian. When I was a boy, many traders came to Klawock for Sea Otter. My father came every summer. Then when there were too few otters to hunt, the traders stopped coming." Then sadly he said, "My father never came back."

He took another sip. "Enough talk. Now we eat."

And so it went. For the moment they were safe but they knew it was just a matter of time before they would be discovered. As days turned to weeks, and winter to spring, they watched many Haida canoes pass by their beach to hunt, fish, and to war. The Haida always came from the east where the water turned north into Cordova Bay. Kloo raised his arm and pointed south across Dixon Entrance. "They came here a long way from across the water. Our people have lived here since the beginning. The Haida, they are newcomers and we allowed them to stay here. The land is big. Enough room for both our peoples to live in peace but instead they choose war."

Six months before the day Vincent found Kloo on the beach, the Haida raided Klawock and took Kloo's daughter and some of the villagers as prisoners; slaves. Now all that was on Kloo's mind was to rescue his people. He pleaded for Vincent's help and Vincent agreed.

They needed to plan. And they did.

So a few nights later under a full moon they made their way through the concealing shadows of the forest fringe. To the northeast across Kaigani Straight on the shore of Long Island they saw the light of a large fire.

Kloo spat on the ground then whispered, "Haida's Howkan village."

Keeping to the shadows they walked another mile or so until they were directly across from the village. The fire illuminated the narrow channel between them and the village. They stayed in the forest and watched.

There must have been at least a hundred natives dancing and singing. Nearby the Tlingit prisoners sat on the ground tied and hobbled.

Kloo whispered, "The Haidas, they drink Russian hooch."

Their plan was simple. They assumed that by the end of the night everyone in the village would be asleep or too drunk to see straight. In essence, they would swim across the narrow channel then sneak past the drunken guards and free the prisoners. Then they would sneak back to the beach where the Haida canoes were lined up. They'd escape in two of the canoes after setting fire to the rest and paddle up along the east coast of Dall Island and head back to Klawock; if the weather cooperated and traveling only at night, they should be back to their village in less than a week.

The question was how to get across the narrow channel? The water was cold and deep and Kloo couldn't swim.

About that time, fate stepped in. Three natives could be seen moving from the campfire; two men and a woman. The woman, about the size of Kloo, was being dragged with a noose tied around her neck to one of the beached canoes.

Kloo rose and almost yelled, "My daughter Mila!"

Vincent placed his hand on Kloo's shoulder. "Sh." They both sat back down.

The woman struggled as best she could but the two men just laughed and pulled her into the canoe with them. Paddler in the bow and stern and Mila between; they headed toward the two rescuers who waited quietly in the darkness.

They beached their canoe less than fifty feet from Kloo and Vincent and then dragged the terrified woman to a place on the beach where she lay "hog-tied" awaiting her death while her captors busied themselves gathering wood to build a fire.

Vincent and Kloo recognized Mila's captors as two of the guards from that day on the beach in front of the cave. Kloo whispered, "Now this is our time."

The Haidas wandered close to the two rescuers. The hooch made them unsteady on their feet and dulled their senses. They were focused on gathering firewood and unaware that Kloo and Vincent waited patiently at the forest edge just a few feet above them.

Kloo pointed to the one to the right. That was the one who had beaten Kloo and left him to die. And now, he belonged to Kloo. As the two Haidas bent to collect kindling, the two stalkers pounced from the shadows. Their clubs crushed the unsuspecting guard's skulls in quick fashion. Not so much as a grunt from either of them; one moment they were alive and the next, dead.

Kloo turned back to his daughter and set her free. Theirs was a joyous tearful momentary embrace. Calm and coordinated, Vincent and Kloo hid the bodies deep in the forest being especially careful not to leave a trace.

Mila said soon the powerful Chief Sukal from Kasaan was coming with his warriors to join with the Haida at Howkan. He was going to lead a raiding party south across Dixon Entrance to plunder the Tsimpsean villages on the Queen Charolette Islands.

Kloo told Vincent, "Chief Sukal is the most feared of all Kaigani chiefs. He has many warriors and muskets. The Tlingit slaves at Howkan will be spared while the raiding party is away killing and taking more prisoners. But when the Haida return, the Tlingits will be killed and eaten."

There was no time to waste so the three survivors quickly left that place and paddled back to Cape Muzon and the safety of their cave where they would make another plan.

For the next two days they watched Haida search parties looking for the two warriors. The cave was cold but for fear of detection, no fires were made. Once a group of searchers came ashore just down the beach and went up into the forest. If they ever found the canoe hidden close by, they would find the cave.

Then after an hour or so the Haida reappeared back on the beach. From time to time while they talked they pointed towards the forest nearby the cave. Apparently some of them wanted to continue the search while others objected. In the end, and to the survivor's relief, they decided to leave.

That was the last search party the three ever saw. Then two days later, the morning stillness was broken by musket fire coming from the direction of Howkan. A few hours later, Haida war canoes appeared southbound across Dixon Entrance. In a week or two they would return. Until they did, Howkan would be a village of old men, women, children, and the Tlingit prisoners.

21

RESCUE

Late at night under an overcast sky the three beached their canoe in line with seven others. There were no sentries. Mila pointed to the hut where the prisoners were kept. The sendoff celebration that day left the old guard at the doorway in a drunken stupor. He sat on the ground with his back propped against the door frame, legs splayed out in the direction of the dying fire, and a jug of hooch at his side. One blow from Kloo's club insured the guard wouldn't be a problem.

Inside the hut the five Tlingits sat on the floor. Ankles hobbled, arms tied behind their backs, and bound by their necks to heavy cedar posts. All five were asleep.

Kloo kept one hand over each one's mouth as he carefully woke one after the other; "sh, my brother. It is I, Kloo. We are here to rescue you."

A moment or two later Kloo asked, "What happened to the others?"

"Chief Sukal shot them."

There was no time to waste. As they left the hut Vincent bent down and took the dead guard's drink; "might as well take it." Silently the eight of them retraced their steps out of the sleeping village back to the canoes.

Kloo said, "We take two canoes. There is no time to waste. Push the others into the channel and let the current take them away."

With two canoes and provisions from their cave, the seven Tlingits and Vincent made their escape. By sunrise they had left Howkan far behind and were riding an incoming spring tide northward up Kaigani Straight.

With no canoes and their warriors gone to plunder there would be no Haida search party. At least until Chief Sukal returned.

Later that morning the scene at Howkan was pure pandemonium. Someone found the dead guard and sounded the alarm. "The Tlingits have escaped." Their canoes couldn't be found and their warriors were away. What to do? What to do?

The shaman was summoned.

They cried to him, "How could this happen?"

The shaman answered, "It was a bad omen the night the spirits took our two warriors (thanks to Vincent and Kloo). As proof, the prisoners have been freed."

He looked into the crowd. "Someone here has angered the great spirit."

A terrified young girl, not more than fifteen years old, was pushed forward. The week before she had intercourse with a cousin and both were of the same Ravens clan; strictly taboo. She begged for forgiveness.

The buried her and her unborn fetus alive and above her head they planted a cedar sapling. The shaman turned to the frightened villagers and said, "The evil demon in this girl will be trapped in this tree for as long as it shall live."

He turned to the heavens. "We call on you great spirit to keep this tree alive and strong and accept the body of this child as our sacrifice!"

22

ESCAPE

On sheer adrenaline they paddled for the rest of the day. Then towards sundown they beached the two canoes in a cove at the north end of Dall Island just south of a place called Tlevak (pronounced Klevak) Narrows.

Kloo pointed to the channel, "too much danger now to enter the narrows. We set up camp for the night."

The eight of them sat by the fire and shared Kloo's leftover soup along with a swig or two of the hooch.

One young fellow spoke, "We should have killed them in their sleep." The young men agreed.

Someone said, "We should have honored our dead brothers and killed the Kaigani. Instead we left like cowards."

Then Kloo spoke, "My young brothers, I have listened to you." He paused, "You were in no shape to fight! There were too many in that village. If we did as you say and killed a few, only to have been killed, then no one in our village would have known our fate or about Chief Sukal. Revenge at the cost of our lives would gain us nothing. We will return to Klawock and tell our story to the council and our justice will come."

One young man named Kvas stood and without emotion turned and walked away. The four others followed. After an hour or so they returned to the fire. Kvas stood before Kloo and said, "Because of you we are alive. For that we are grateful."

Kloo put his hand on the young man's shoulder, "Then tomorrow we go home to tell our story." The tide was shifting and Vincent could see up ahead a huge whirlpool develop in the center of the channel. He watched the trunk of a tall cedar tree that had washed off the beach, drift into the vortex and then disappear. Sucked down beneath the surface and then minutes later it bobbed back up a half mile from where it was pulled under.

Kloo said, "When the tide is slack, there is no whirlpool. We can pass through the narrows tomorrow morning."

Later that night Mila and Vincent were alone together. The twinkling stars, like grains of sand on the beach, too numerous to count, spread across a velvet sky. A soft spring breeze filled the air with the fragrance of the cedar forest.

Mila's hand touched Vincent's and she whispered, "Gunalcheesh (thank you)."

He kissed her gently and said, "You're welcome."

At sunrise the following morning, Vincent and the Tlingits left their campsite. As Kloo had predicted, Tlevak Narrows was glassy calm and they passed through with ease. They were safe in Tlingit country. Up Ulloa Channel, past San Juan Bautista Island, Fish Egg Island, and then finally a few hours later they entered Klawock Inlet.

At the end of the inlet and well protected by mountains on three sides lies Klawock Bay. Kloo pointed to the small Tlingit village of Klawock and spoke, "for many summers, too many to count, our people came here from their northern winter camp. As it had always been done, fish are caught, smoked, and salted and used throughout the rest of the year; everyone: man; woman; and child takes part in the harvest." Life was good at summer camp and eventually, Klawock became a permanent village.

As they paddled up the inlet, sentries alerted the town. "Kloo, Kloo. It is Kloo who returns with our people."

The villagers gathered on the beach and as the canoes came ashore, there was a great show of happiness for the survivors and grief for the lost.

One young man stepped forward and first embraced Mila and then Kloo. Tears fell from Kloo's eyes. The young man said, "It is good to have you back father."

And Kloo said, "It is good to be back, my son."

The survivors were then escorted to a central longhouse. There were at least a dozen communal houses in the village but this was the largest; at least seventy feet long and thirty feet wide and constructed with massive posts and beams and covered throughout with split log planks; all of Red Cedar. The carved poles outside the narrow entrance announced that this house belonged to the Raven moiety. It was where the chief and his family stayed. It was also the central meeting place for the village.

Inside the building at its far side, opposite the entry, Chief Yas and his council of nine elders sat atop a cedar plank platform raised above the recessed dirt floor. He held an intricately carved Yellow Cedar staff at his side and all wore magnificent regalia. Chilkat robes woven from cedar bark and mountain goat hair and trimmed with white ermine fur. Spruce root head gear. Nose and lip rings of abalone "mother of pearl." And their bodies were abundantly decorated with tattoos of various abstract designs.

To the rear of the platform, a cedar plank wall screen stretched almost the full width of the room. It was carved in shallow relief and embellished with a multitude of clan crests and abstract figures that spoke Tlingit history and legend. Standing on either side of the screen were massive carved cedar posts.

The Tlingit people had no written alphabet so they recorded their history in their carvings. The fragrant aroma inside that building was like that of a cedar chest.

Yas was an old chief; possibly in his seventies. Even so, his tattooed, six foot tall, battle scarred frame made him an imposing figure. He was a wise chief, proven in battle and respected by enemy and friend alike. He was a man of few words and when he spoke, all listened.

The survivors stood, heads bowed, before the platform. Kloo raised his head and spoke, "My Chief, many tides ago we were taken away from our home and enslaved by the Haida. They murdered our brothers and would have killed us all had it not been for this man who stands at my side, my friend Ven-sant. Because of him we stand before you tonight. And because of him many Tlingit children are yet to be born."

All was quiet, while Chief Yas spoke. "Ven-sant, we thank you for the return of our people. Those who have died have not done so in vain. The Tlingit will forever be in your debt. We ask you to consider Klawock your home and our people your family." With that he stepped from the platform, gave each of the survivors a reassuring grip, and then signaled the servants who were standing at a side door.

Plates of food were brought in and while they ate, the council asked Kloo many questions: how they escaped; did they kill any Haida; how many warriors went with Chief Sukal; how many were left in the village; and were there any slaves left at Howkan.

As for Vincent, the Tlingit were well-aquainted with the dark haired swarthy Russians, but this light skinned blonde American was different. With Kloo as their translator, they asked him how he came to their part of the world, the wreck of the Thomas B, his survival, and his rescue of Kloo.

The questions and answers continued and then one of the council stood. "My son Koosh died at the hands of the Kaigani. Why Kloo, when you had the chance, why didn't you kill more of the Haida? Was my son not worthy of revenge?"

All eyes were on Kloo. After a moment or two he rose and said, "My brother, we are all of the same family. Your son Koosh was as a son to me as are all the young men of our village. What wounds one, wounds all. What one suffers, all suffer. It is the nature of our community. We are all tied together as one."

Before the man could answer, Kloo raised his palm and added, "My friend it was no time for a revenge that would only burn as a flash of tinder in the absence of more wood. It was our responsibility to bring our story back to you." Koosh's father bowed his head in silence.

Chief Yas announced, "Enough talk for now. Tomorrow we will decide our revenge."

That night Vincent stayed at Kloo's house along with Kloo's aunts, uncles, cousins and others of the Dog Salmon clan. To say the least, the women and children were fascinated by Vincent. Every once in a while a hand would reach out to touch him or stroke his hair. It was obvious though that Vincent wasn't quite sure how to react so Kloo announced that while his friend was a guest in their house he should be treated with respect. And just to make sure Vincent felt comfortable, Mila stayed by his side. She made it clear that he was not an eligible bachelor.

Kloo was an excellent story teller. Everyone sat perfectly silent, as he recounted, with a modicum of embellishment, details of the daring rescue and narrow escape. An hour or so later, and that version of the story finished, Kloo said, "Our journey has come to an end and now it is time to go to sleep."

Kloo's son turned to Vincent. "I am Go-nish, the son of Kloo. Thank you for saving my father."

He was considerably larger than his father; with a strong muscular build and his face (framed by his long thick coal black hair), not typically native but was refined somewhat by his European ancestry. Here was a young man that would someday be chief.

A corner of the room had been prepared for Vincent. And for his privacy, a Black Bear rug was hung from the ceiling in front of the sleeping mat. Mila lay down beside him. He looked at her and she whispered, "To keep the other women away."

Vincent smiled and they slept in each other's embrace.

23

TLINGIT REVENGE

A grand potlatch was thrown the next day in the central longhouse to celebrate the survivor's return to Klawock and to mourn brothers lost. Dancers in their ornate tunics and leggings beat their deerskin drums and shook their rattles. They sang their songs and performed intricate ceremonial dances that celebrated both folklore and history.

It was exciting to watch and at the conclusion of the entertainment Vincent was embraced as a hero, and officially welcomed into the tribe.

Chief Yas spoke to the guests of honor. "Kloo, once again you have proven yourself wise and brave." He turned to Vincent, "From this day on your Tlingit name will be Tsala ("one that returns").

Later that night, Chief Yas met with his council. "Chief Sukal and his warriors have gone recently to plunder tribes across the great water to the south. This we know because Kloo chose to bring us this information. In his greed and overconfidence Sukal has left his village in Kasaan weak and unprotected. So we will go there. We will take the Sea Otter pelts that fill his storehouse. And we will free his slaves. His anger will be great and cause him to come after us. This will be his great mistake. The time has come for us to pull the teeth of the Haida bear."

Over the next few days, preparations were made for a campaign that would take two hundred of Klawock's strongest warriors, led by Go-nish, to Kasaan village.

Go-nish took his seat in the central longhouse alongside his troops. Then Chief Yas summoned the shaman to invoke the spirits to protect and insure these young warriors a victorious defeat of the Haida. Standing in the center of the floor, the painted shaman stood with his arms spread. He shook his rattles and moved his body back and forth in trancelike fashion while repeating his chant over and over: "Nu-ah-ta, Nu-ah-ta, Nu-ah-ta. Ah-naash-cheesh; Nu-a-ta, Nu-a-ta, Nu-a-ta. Ahnaash-cheesh."

The Shaman turned to Go-nish and while the young man knelt, the old mystic shook his rattle again and poured his magical potion onto Go-nish's head and shoulders. More chanting followed. The shaman waved his eagle feather across the cheering warriors and then backed out of the longhouse. Everyone seemed satisfied that the spirits were now on their side and victory was theirs.

The next morning, cleansed and invigorated, Go-nish and his warriors emerged from their sweat lodges. They were ready. Chief Yas spoke to the young warriors, "your moment to bring honor to you village is at hand. This will be a time that will live on in Tlingit legend; may the spirits look upon you with pride."

Go-nish embraced his father and sister and then turned to Vincent. "Thank you."

As the crowd wept and cheered, Go-nish led his warriors out of the village.

Kasaan village lay due east on the opposite side of the island. The fifty mile trek there would lead them across lakes, rivers, mountainous terrain, and dense forest. A grueling journey well suited for the eager young Tlingits.

On the last night of their seven day forced march they were camped within a mile of their goal. As expected, their scouts reported only a few warriors in the village. So, early the next morning before the Haida began to stir, the Tlingit attacked. Go nish gave strict orders, "kill none of the unarmed villagers."

It was complete mayhem. Dogs barked and the villagers cried out in fear, while the half- naked screaming Tlingit warriors in war paint and regalia, and brandishing war clubs and muskets terrorized the village. Surprise attacks are so effective. The Haida warriors left to guard Chief Sukal's storehouse were killed.

Women grabbed their children and babies and ran into the forest. And those left in the village were made to watch Go-nish's warriors burn Chief Sukal's lodge. They freed the slaves and later left with a few captured muskets and thirty prisoners to carry the many bales of Sea Otter pelts. Chief Sukal would know the Tlingits were responsible.

As Go-nish and his warriors had been marching on Kasaan, the second prong of a two prong attack began.

That night at the longhouse after the shaman had summoned the spirits to protect Go-nish and his men, Chief Yas turned to Kloo and Vincent and said, "I am too old to fight. You both have proven yourselves to be wise leaders who work well together. Both of you will lead the rest of our warriors to set your trap."

Vincent, Kloo, and fifty Tlingit warriors paddled their way back to Tlevak Narrows. They knew, when Chief Sukal returned to Howkan from his conquests in the Queen Charolette Islands, he would be greeted with details of the Tlingit prisoner's escape as well as the raid on Kasaan village. Chief Sukal would be enraged. And his army of battle hardened Haida warriors fresh from their recent victories would be eager to destroy Klawock and capture more women and slaves.

And the shortest route to achieve that goal would take them through Tlevak Narrows. The bay at the south end of the Narrows was the perfect place to set the trap.

Within the bay was a maze of little forested islands where Vincent and Kloo and their band of Tlingit would hide in ambush.

Chief Sukal and his warriors, chanting their songs of battle and paddling north on an incoming tide would pass into the bay through its south entrance on their way to Klawock. There the little band of Tlingits would antagonize and delay their more powerful foe. And with Mother Nature as their ally plus luck, they would defeat the Haida.

And so, on signal as the Haida were midway through the bay, the Tlingits emerged from their hiding places shooting their muskets and arrows and shouting obscenities.

The ruse worked. As angry as Chief Sukal was when he entered the bay, now he was red faced and shaking with rage. As hard as he tried to engage the Tlingits in battle though, he failed. From one island to the other, as the Haidas beached their canoes in pursuit, the Tlingits would shoot a volley or two and then escape through the forest and paddle off to another island to keep on annoying their pursuers.

Noticing a change in the tide, Chief Sukal called off the pursuit and ordered his warriors to continue on to Klawock. But by the time his canoes were half way through the narrow south entrance, it was too late. Mother Nature entered the battle. As strong as the Haida paddlers were, they could make no headway. The tide was too powerful. The eighty northbound Haida war canoes were stopped by the outgoing southbound current. As much as Chief Sukal screamed at them, it was no use. Their canoes were pushed backwards.

Then as if from nowhere, Go-nish and his warriors appeared on the rocks above the Haida. They fired mercilessly downward into the canoes. The panic stricken Haidas were being slaughtered. Recognizing the hopelessness of his situation, Chief Sukal ordered retreat.

A few of the canoes broached and capsized in the swift current as others were swept out of the narrow channel to disappear into the waiting whirlpool. Vincent and Kloo watched from shore as Chief Sukal and the few canoes that miraculously escaped the vortex were met by agile Tlingit canoes. In the end, four hundred and fifty Haida were killed and thirty, Chief Sukal included, had been captured; total Tlingit loss, six.

It was a fine day for the Tlingit. Vincent, Kloo, Go-nish, and their warriors sang their victory songs as they returned with their prisoners to Klawock. The prisoners were paraded in front of the town and then taken to the central longhouse where Chief Yas and his council would pronounce judgment.

With their hands bound behind them and their ankles hobbled, Chief Sukal and his warriors were forced to kneel in the dirt in front of the platform.

Chief Yas rose from his seat. All were quiet as he spoke, "Many times the Haida have come to our village. Not in peace but to kill and capture our people." He pointed a finger at Chief Sukal and continued, "You have come again, but this time as our prisoner. We have beaten you in battle and from this day forward, the Haida will no longer be feared as a threat."

It was the crafty Chief Sukal's turn to speak. Knowing that his head (literally) was at stake, he began, "The Haida are a proud people. We are feared by many, as far as the eagle flies. Never had I been defeated in battle. Now my warriors are dead; killed by the Tlingit. Our women will mourn and my people are without defense.

Hear me, I do not fear my death but I beg you to spare my people."

Chief Sukal bowed his head and after a prolonged moment of silence, Chief Yas stood. "You speak of mercy. It is you who gave none to those you captured. Know this Chief Sukal, the Tlingit are a proud and just people. But do not confuse kindness with weakness. I say again, the Haida will no longer be feared by our people. A few Tlingit have defeated you and your many warriors."

He paused for a moment then continued, "You will be allowed to return in shame to your people. All prisoners that you have taken, you will release unharmed and allowed to return to their villages. And never again will you wage war on the Tlingit. If you agree to this with solemn word, no harm from us will come to you or your people. We seek peace, not war."

Chief Sukal looked at his terrified warriors and then agreed to Chief Yas's terms.

Chief Yas turned to Go-nish, "Escort the Haida back to Howkan and bring back any of their prisoners that choose to return with you."

That being said, the Haida, heads bowed, were slowly led down to the beach as Tlingit women and children pelted them with sticks and stones. They left under Tlingit escort and never again returned to Klawock as enemies.

24

PEACE

With the Haida no longer a threat, it was a peaceful spring in Klawock. Life in the village was uncomplicated. Just a few reasonable rules, which if broken could mean the difference between acceptance and rejection. Acceptance meant survival while rejection meant being shunned or at worst, exiled. Indeed, for the survival of the community, its members had to contribute to its well-being, and anyone who jeopardized its survival was not tolerated.

In time, Vincent felt at home in Klawock . Here he found meaning. He became fluent in the Tlingit language and his experience and skill as a seaman and boat builder made him a valuable part of the community. He learned the ways of the Tlingit and was adopted into Kloo's family thereby becoming an honorary member of the Dog Salmon clan under the Raven. He fell in love with Mila, and since he wasn't a Raven by blood, they were allowed to marry.

It was time for Vincent and Mila to move from the crowded communal house and raise a family.

One special day Kloo came to Vincent and Mila. "I have something important to show you both."

They paddled their canoe halfway up Klawock Lake to the mouth of Four Mile Creek. It was a beautiful brisk spring morning. The sun was out and the previous night's storm was just a memory. The three of them stood on the river bank and watched a female black bear and her cub graze among the heavily laden salmon berry bushes. Kloo said, "As a wedding present I give you this stream. It has always belonged to our family and as tradition speaks it is now your responsibility to protect. If you do so, it will always provide for you. Every fall, the Dog Salmon will return and they are yours. As they prosper, so will your family."

They built their cabin at the mouth of the creek among the fragrant cedars. They were happy there and in time Mila bore Vincent three fine sons. And Kloo was a proud and caring grandfather.

Life was good. Every summer hordes of salmon returned to Klawock Bay. First to appear were the Reds, then the Pinks, followed by the Silvers, and finally in early Fall came the Dogs. All were bound for Klawock Lake and its tributaries. Each sought out its own natal stream.

Every fall, Mila and Vincent and their boys would trap just enough Dog Salmon from their creek to provide sustenance throughout the coming winter.

25

WINTER

The winter of 1860 was cold, colder than normal, and with it came the sickness; Tuberculosis. To make matters worse, since the people were crowded into their communal houses, the disease quickly spread from one household to the other. No one knew what to do.

One day Vincent came to Kloo and said, "My friend this village is a dangerous place to be. The shaman cannot cure this disease. If you stay here you will most certainly die. Those who are still healthy must move away."

Kloo answered, "The people will not leave their home."

So Vincent placed a hand on Kloo's shoulder and spoke with the same compassion that took Kloo back to the time when they first met, "Then to survive, you must come with me and live with our family where it is safe."

The cold north wind blew; Four Mile Creek was frozen hard; and Kloo and the family stayed warm in their tight little cabin where there was no shortage of salted salmon. During the day Vincent and the boys kept busy collecting firewood, hunting, and checking their trap line.

The surface of the lake was frozen making access to the opposite shore an easy half mile walk. Trapping was especially good on the other side where there was an abundance of mink, wolves, martin, beaver, and ermine. At this time of year, pelts were in prime condition; the colder the weather, the better.

The clear crisp night sky was magical. Along with a bright moon and billions of stars that carpeted the heavens were the Northern Lights; intermittent flashes of green and blue illuminations in part due to solar wind particles colliding with atmospheric nitrogen and oxygen atoms. It is called the Aurora Borealis and some simply said, "It is the dance of the spirits." And the frozen stillness was broken now and then by the sorrowful howling of wolves from across the lake.

26

A TOTEM FOR VINCENT

One day Kloo told Vincent, "Twice you have saved my life. The time has come for me to carve a pole for you. It will tell the history of you and our family for all to see long after we are gone. It will tell how you came to us and what you have done. It will be there for all to know."

After a thoughtful pause he continued, "The boys will help me and when it is done we will stand it near the mouth of the stream for all to see."

Surrounding beautiful Klawock Lake was an ancient evergreen forest of spruce, hemlock, and cedar; centuries old giants.

Each has a character of its own. True, spruce and hemlock have excellent load bearing qualities suitable for heavy construction. But it is the fragrant Red Cedar that carvers choose. Straight fine grained, lightweight, and resistant to rot.

Not far from the cabin, Kloo pointed to an old red giant. "This tree will make a fine pole." The tree was at least two hundred feet tall and four feet in diameter. It took all day to chop it down and then cut off the thirty foot length that would be their totem pole.

Over the following days the tree was prepared for carving. First the limbs were removed and next to go was the thick outer bark exposing the rich aromatic crimson colored inner wood; pliable and moist and perfect for the task ahead.

They squared off one side of the log; the back of the pole. And then as if building a dugout canoe, Kloo stood on the flat surface and while bent over with his feet spread apart he swung his iron adze as if it were a pendulum. Over and over and sometimes just narrowly missing his feet, he guided the blade into the wood, downward, back and forth.

The boys stood transfixed as their grandfather worked. At one point, the old man allowed the boys, under his careful tutelage, to take their turns and get the feel of the wood. This was the native way.

Centuries of growth was accounted for as the pile of chips grew. And as Kloo and the boys moved down the log the furrow grew deeper and deeper until finally, after a week or so, the log was reduced to a thick shell, ready for carving.

Among his talents, Kloo was a fine Tlingit carver. First, in charcoal he would draw his designs on the log. And then when satisfied with what he had done, from his buckskin pouch he brought out his "special" razor sharp knives and adzes and began to teach the boys to carve.

Each figure was a complexity of ovals, u's, and s's; the three essential elements of northwest coast native design. Each cut had to be a certain depth and at a certain angle. His art was not interpretive "free form," but rigid "traditional."

He said, "my grandfather taught me to carve as I am now teaching you." He would hold out a knife and touch it to the wood. "You hold it like this."

Then with one quick sweeping motion of his wrist away from his body he would remove a flake of wood. The shape of the flake reflected the shape of the blade. Hook or straight edge, each element of the design required a different blade.

The boys copied his example. At first they were given simple tasks. Kloo would say, "Okay, just follow this line. Not too deep. Now gouge this out. Not too far. Okay, that's good. Now do this. Now do that. Good job."

He was a patient teacher and the boys learned. And the aroma was wonderful.

That was a time for telling stories as it was the carver who brought history and legends to life. It was also the time to pass on knowledge. As they carved he told the story of each figure. He would say for example, "This is· Raven who created the world and made the forests, mountains, rivers, and sea. It was Raven who gave man knowledge and brought him the light, the stars, and the moon."

It was an exciting time for the boys. They were fully engaged in the work and eager to learn. Each morning the young apprentices would go with their grandfather into the forest and return home at dark. And by the time the pole was finished, the winter was over and they were proud of what they had accomplished.

27

A NEW BEGINNING

By spring, disease had left the village along with a quarter of its population; including Chief Yas. A three day potlatch was held for the chief and the others. The villagers mourned for two weeks and then as if on cue, life in the village returned to normal; time marched on.

Go-nish became chief and Kloo remained with Vincent and his family at Four Mile Creek.

One day a ship came to Klawock. The men weren't Russians from Sitka but were representatives from Washington. The men told Go-nish and his people that Russia sold Alaska to the United States and that the Tlingit were now Americans.

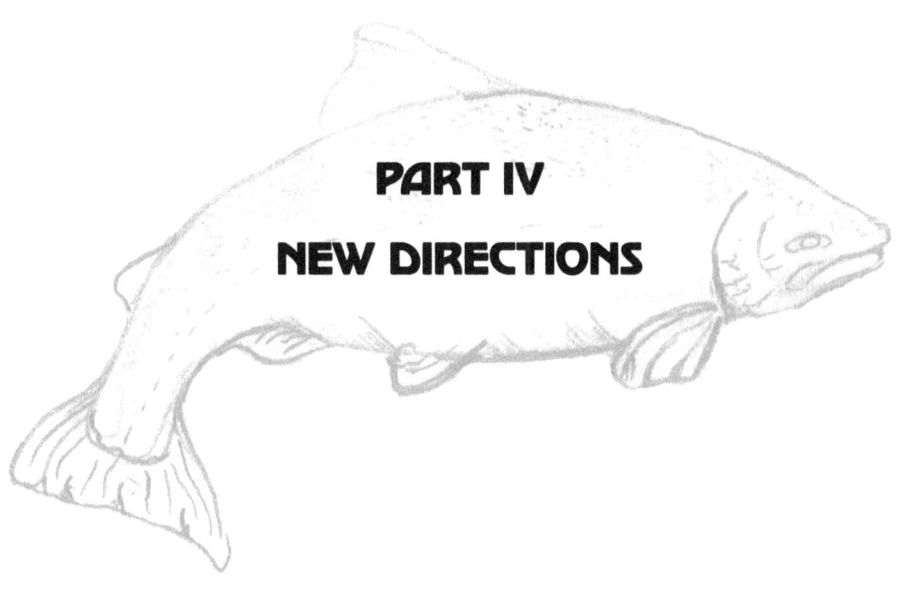

PART IV
NEW DIRECTIONS

28

RETURN FROM THE *SEA*

I was totally content just to sit there on that pile of web out on the back deck of the Mary Ann surrounded by Mother Nature in all her glory. Bone tired but in my heart I knew, commercial fishing was something I could do for as long as I was able. I was hooked. Even Double Shot was smiling. Noyes Island was behind us and we were returning to Klawock.

By eleven o'clock that night we tied up to the cannery, along with ten other seine boats waiting to offload. Everyone waited their turn. All went smooth and by two o'clock the next morning we left the cannery and were approaching the Klawock dock.

Just inches before colliding with the float, the gears were shifted into reverse and the Mary Ann came to a stop. Then after a series of delicate maneuvers she was broadside to the dock and parked with little room to spare between the steel seine boat in front and a fiberglass yacht in back. It would have been bad if we dented the seiner but really bad if we crushed the yacht. Ben and I jumped onto the dock and secured our lines. Marvin was happy. "Tie off those lines boys."

That done he said, "You did good, boys. Looks like Saturday's going to be our next opening."

Double Shot and Too Tall drew their pay and headed for Craig's Inn. Marvin turned to Ben and me, "You boys want to come home with me?"

The Selkirk home was a large three story house overlooking the harbor. It was their home now and in its colorful past the one hundred year old structure had first been a post office and later a hotel. Mavin's grandfather barged it from Howkan after the town was abandoned in 1911 and Marvin, along with his five brothers were raised in this house.

As we walked through the front door a voice summoned us into the kitchen. There Marvin's wife Mary, coffee pot in hand, smiled and said, "Come in gentlemen."

We took our places at the table. She filled our cups and passed us a heaping plate full of toasted homemade bread. On the table was salmonberry jam, and butter. Life is good.

Framed pictures hung on the walls: family; friends; and fishing boats. There was a cork bulletin board and pinned to it were other snapshots (dogs, cats, flowers, children, etc.), pieces of paper with names and telephone numbers, and various other memorabilia. And in the center of it all were the colored ribbons that were the scholastic and athletic awards of their four grandchildren.

To one side of the cork board hung a calendar. Memos tacked under its various dates were notices of council meetings, doctor's appointments, and choir practice. The one under July 21st read, "Call Dorothy/Sissy."

Marvin's voice re-focused my attention. "Mary, this is Dylan. Dylan this is my wife Mary."

I held out my hand, smiled, and said, "It's nice to meet you Mrs. Selkirk."

She took my hand. "It's nice to meet you too Dylan. You boys must be tired."

I shook my head. "Yes mam, a little," and added, "You must be tired too."

She answered politely, "Not too. I've been doing this for a long time. It's just part of the life of a fisherman's wife."

One things for sure, the moment I met Mary I liked her.

Marvin finished his toast; drained his cup and said, "Think I'll turn in. Ben show Dylan where he's going to sleep." He paused. "See you all in the morning," then turned to Mary. "Don't be too hard on the boy." With that Marvin left the room.

Ben set his empty cup down and yawned.

Mary turned to him. "Go to bed son, I'll show Dylan his room."

As I was about to stand Mary motioned me to stay seated. So over another cup of coffee, we talked. It was more of an informal and friendly interrogation that covered my past, present, and future. And when it was through I asked, "Did I pass?"

She smiled. "Yes, you passed."

Then she said, "I understand you met Dorothy's daughter, Sissy." I nodded, "yes that's right."

"Well, what do you think about her?"

I told her how I felt and she smiled. After a thoughtful pause I changed the subject and asked her about herself.

Somewhat surprised and somewhat pleased that I asked, she answered, "Well, not much to tell but when I was a teenager, during World War Two, I came here with my father. He was an army engineer who helped build the airport and other projects around southeast Alaska. I met Marvin and we fell in love and got married. And so for better or worse, I became a fisherman's wife." She smiled.

She went on to say, not long after they were married, Marvin inherited their house after his father and three brothers drowned when their fishing boat sank.

She sighed, "It was one night during a winter storm off Noyes Island. They said a plank under the water line sprung loose and the boat sank in minutes." Then, "It was a cold winter."

"I'm sorry to hear that," I said.

"Thanks. That was a long time ago. A lot of water has passed under the bridge. And we've been blessed. Our four children were born and raised in this home. Ben is the youngest and the only boy. The girls have families of their own and we're grandparents."

She smiled and then pointed to a snapshot on the bulletin board, "there."

It was a Christmas card photo of Marvin and Mary, their four children, and seven little grandchildren (infants, toddlers, and pre-teens) grouped together on the deck of the Mary Ann with the big house in the background. Underneath the happy scene, the words read: "Merry Christmas from the Selkirks."

Mary paused. She appeared troubled. I asked if something was wrong.

She lowered her voice, "Well, I'm afraid Marvin is getting too old to run the Mary Ann. He doesn't want to stop fishing but he knows it's about time to turn the boat over to Ben."

She paused again then asked, "You think Ben is ready?"

I felt uneasy. "I think you're asking the wrong person but from what I've seen, I do."

She stood and smiled, "Dylan, I'm glad we've had this little talk. Let me show you to your room."

I glanced again at the note on the calendar under July 21st and was glad I passed Mary's interrogation.

29

A NEW DAY

I longed for a hot shower, clean sheets, and sleep. It seemed to me that I had just closed my eyes and then presto, it was seven o'clock in the morning. I wandered downstairs to the kitchen and took my place at the table with Ben, Marvin, and Too Tall.

Marvin asked, "So Mary, what do you think of Dylan?"

Her answer, "He passed."

They all laughed.

Mary turned from the stove carrying a plate of steaming hot cakes. "Good morning Dylan. Hope you slept well."

I poured myself a cup of coffee. "Good morning and yes mam I did."

About that time we all looked up as Bobby and Dorothy Thomas walked in.

Bobby said, "I thought we'd come over and fish Tuesday's opening off Addington and Sumez."

Marvin stood then shook Bobby's hand and asked, "So when'd ya get in?"

"We pulled into Craig about six this morning. Nappy and the rest of the crew are on board patching gear. They should be done soon."

Mary and Dorothy hugged each other warmly after months and miles of separation.

With tears in her eyes, Mary as the gracious host pointed to the table and said, "You're just in time for breakfast." Then, "Sit down, sit down."

It was an excellent Saturday morning breakfast at the Selkirks.

Bobby reached for the syrup and announced, "I talked with Barry Stahl last night. He said he's got engine problems but was gonna try and meet us at Steamboat.

Ben snickered, "I bet he's already there waiting for us."

Dorothy's attention was directed to Dylan's pancake laden fork temporarily frozen in mid-air between his plate and mouth. Obviously, Bobby's news caught his attention.

She smiled, "Yes Dylan, Sissy said she missed you and was looking forward to seeing you there."

Dylan could feel a warm flush cross his face. He looked at Marvin and said, "If it's okay with you skipper, I'd like to take off a little early."

Marvin smiled, "Dylan, take the seine skiff and meet us at Steamboat. We'll see you tomorrow night."

Marvin looked over at Too Tall, who had been battling a hangover from the previous night in Craig. "Where's Double Shot?"

Too Tall raised the sunglasses off his face to reveal a pair of deep purple and black welts (shiners). "The last time I saw him he was being hauled off to jail."

Ben asked, "What happened?"

Too Tall poured himself a second cup of coffee. "Oh don't worry, he's okay. But I'm not sure about the other guys. That's the last time I'm goin' to Craig's Inn. I swear." A short pause then, "At least until the end of the season."

Marvin folded his arms, stared straight ahead, and speaking to no one in particular said, "I don't care if he is the best skiff man in southeast. With or without him we're leaving tomorrow.

30

STEAMBOAT BAY

By nine o'clock that morning Dylan was in the seine skiff and heading for Steamboat Bay. By noon the weather had turned from sunny, clear and calm to overcast with a westerly blowing at twenty five knots.

The wind and choppy sea had slowed him considerably but for Dylan it was Sissy and not the weather that was on his mind. And by the time he arrived at the bay, it was six o'clock that evening and the wind had picked up to forty knots. Inside the bay it was dead calm.

Dylan tied up to the cannery dock. The only other boat in the bay was the seiner Silver Gem.

The screen door slammed behind Dylan as he walked into the cannery office. There, George Franco, sitting at his desk with a smoldering cigar stub stuck in the comer of his mouth looked up and asked, "What ya need?"

Dylan answered, "Well sir, I'm looking for the Harvester."

George said nonchalantly, "Oh, they pulled out of here around ten this morning."

Dylan, somewhat confused, asked, "Did they say where they were going?"

By this time George was definitely irritated by the questions. He paused, took the cigar stub from his mouth, spat into an empty pop can and said, "North."

On his way out Dylan could feel something was seriously wrong. It just didn't make sense. He thought, "There's no way Barry would bring his boat all the way from Sitka just to turn around and go back without leaving word. This guy's lying!"

Dylan turned before walking out and said, "Guess I'll see them next time."

The screen door slammed. George whispered, "Yeah, you do that."

At the bottom of wooden steps he met two fishermen from the Silver Gem. He asked, "You guys seen the Harvester?"

The answer was, "Yeah. It pulled out of here around nine this morning."

"Did you see which way it headed?"

The answer was, "South."

Then after a pause one of the fishermen added, "It was towing the cannery's twenty foot cabin cruiser."

Now, Dylan knew something was definitely wrong. He thought to himself, "Well, guess I'll just have to catch them and find out what's going on. That cabin cruiser ought to slow them down."

31

BACK TO BUSINESS

George Franco, alone in his office sat back in his chair and stared out the window watching Dlyan in the seine skiff exit the bay. "Could be trouble," he thought.

About that time the phone rang. George picked it up. "Yes sir, your two men arrived yesterday."

"No sir, Sam hasn't arrived yet."

"Yes sir, we're taking care of the problem."

"Yes sir, thank you sir," and then George hung up the phone.

Within an hour, a single engine float plane appeared. It circled twice then landed at the far end of the bay and taxied up to the dock. The pilot stepped down from the cockpit and moored the plane to the float. Then two men stepped out of the passenger cabin.

George rose from his seat as the two new arrivals entered the office. He said, "I'm glad to see ya Sam, been worried you wouldn't make it here before the fleet arrives."

Sam was the tall slender one that was dressed like a fisherman: red rubber boots; jeans; long sleeved flannel shirt, vest, and a baseball hat with the word "Sonics" emblazoned across its front. "Yeah George, I woulda' been here sooner but we had to pick up this guy in Seattle. He's Lee Wang's replacement."

The passenger was at least ten years older than Sam. He had the look of a timid grocery store manager softened by too many years of city life. He was balding, wore steel framed glasses, black leather shoes, slacks, and was obviously nervous about being here.

The little man held out a soft white hand. "Glad to meet you sir."

Ignoring the gesture, George, upset, turned to Sam, "Who the hell is this guy?"

Sam held up the palm of his right hand, "Alto man, alto! Don't worry, he's okay. He's a real pharmacist. He borrowed some money from the company and couldn't pay it back. So they gave him an alternative, "Work for us or die."

For the past twenty five years, Howard Finley was the owner/operator of Finley's Drug Emporium in Seattle. It was a small family owned business that was suffering from under funding and over competition. In order to survive the competitive edge of the large mega drug stores, Howard had to expand his business, modernize, add floor space, and increase inventory. But that required money and he was already leveraged way past his ability to repay any more loans. The banks turned their backs on him; added to that were the mounting medical bills of his bed ridden wife.

Now, Howard had a friend, Jack, who had a friend, who was a loan shark for Hong Kong Ltd. Import/Export. Their meeting went something like this:

Loan Shark: "So ya wanna borrow some money?"

Howard: "Yes sir."

Loan Shark: "How much?"

Howard: "Three hundred thousand dollars."

Loan Shark: "What's it for?"

Howard: "I need the money to expand my business. Then I'll be able to stay in business and make a profit. But the banks won't loan me any more money."

Loan Shark: "Sorry to hear that Mr. Finley." He paused then said, "If we loan you the money you'll have to pay it back at ten percent per month. That's thirty K per month plus principal."

Howard: "Yes sir I understand."

And that's how Howard Finley became indebted to Hong Kong Ltd Import/Export.

The three stared out the window and watched their pilot open the plane's oversized belly cargo compartment and offload Howard's baggage and a dozen or so large cardboard boxes labeled, "oranges."

Sam turned to George and said with a smirk, "Fresh product needs a little tender loving cutting and then it'll be ready for market." Then he asked, "Ya got something for me?"

George handed Sam a fat envelope. Sam opened it and counted the money.

"Okay George, looks like it's all here. Be sure nothing happens to Howard and I'll see ya in a week."

With that said, Sam turned and walked out the door. Five minutes later, the small plane with its one passenger was airborne and gone.

George turned to Howard. "You'll be here till we don't need you no more. Do what you're told and you'll be just fine."

He pointed to the boxes on the dock. "Now your first job is to move those boxes up to the lab. I'll show you where. My brother Al's gonna be your boss. He's away on business now but will be back later."

32

DARK CLOUDS

With his hands and feet tied, Barry lay face up on the aft deck of the Harvester. His head throbbed and was streaked with dried blood from a three inch gash along its right side. Angie and Sissy were similarly bound and face down on either side of him. David James and John Geeser lay next to the starboard rail. With the wire garrote still around his neck, John was definitely dead. David was alive but just barely.

Best as Barry could recall the day started out as normal. They had tied up at the cannery dock around three o'clock that morning. They were the only boat in the bay. Just after they docked, he had to break up a fight between David and John.

Apparently David discovered John's bag of cocaine that was hidden in the galley and threw it overboard. John was so enraged that he stabbed David in the back. He would have stabbed David again had it not been for Barry.

The fight was over in a matter of seconds. At six foot three and two hundred and twenty pounds, Barry was a powerhouse. He grabbed John by the back of his overalls, spun him around, and threw him up against the cast iron stove.

At most John weighed one hundred and fifty pounds and was a head shorter than Barry. As soon as John hit the stove he collapsed onto the deck. Then Barry turned his attention to David who was bleeding badly. He tried to console his wounded friend. "You're gonna be okay David. We'll get you back to Klawock." He put a dish rag on the wound and told David to hold it there.

About that time Sissy and Angie rushed into the galley to aid David. While they were occupied with David, John regained consciousness and escaped out the door, onto the dock, and headed into the cannery.

Barry said, "You two girls stay here, I'm going after that little bastard!"

He caught John in the lab holding a clear plastic bag half filled with white powder and standing next to the cabinet he had just forced open. Barry was beyond angry. John just held the bag out and stammered, "I'm sorry, please don't hurt me. Here take it. It's coke. You can have it. There's lots of it here."

One swat of Barry's hand and a florescent white cloud exploded into the moonlit room. Too much of a coward to face Barry in a fair fight, John was so scared he began to shake. He was pathetic.

Barry was just about to grab him when the light went on. Standing at the switch was Al Franco and two oversized Chinese thugs armed with large caliber automatics.

Al said, "Well, looky looky what have we here. What-da-ya say boys, we all go talk with the boss, huh." He snatched the baggy from John's hand and grinned, "He'll be real interested in you."

Minutes later, they marched into the cannery office.

George looked up from his paperwork. Without saying a word, he took the partially chewed cigar butt from the corner of his mouth and crushed it into the packed ash tray on the edge of his desk. He stared at the dying ember for a moment then leaned back into his chair, smiled and said, "Relax boys, have a seat." He pointed to the two folding chairs in front of his desk.

With the two armed guards standing behind them Barry and John sat down.

Al handed the plastic bag to George who examined it for a moment or two then smiled and said, "Hmm, looks like someone's been into my coke. You might not think so but this, is my lucky day" (he emphasized the word my).

He looked at Barry and said, "I know you, you're Barry Stahl; owner of the Harvester and a damned good fisherman. You came up the hard way. My hat's off to you. Too bad for you, this isn't your lucky day."

Then he said to John. "As for you my stupid friend, you saved us a lot of trouble. We thought we'd have to hunt you down and then bingo, here you are."

John attempted to stand up but a heavy hand on his shoulder forced him back down in his seat.

Barry interrupted, "Look, I'm not sure what you think happened in that building but I'm not a thief."

"Very interesting, exactly what were you doing in there?"

Looking first to John then back to George he said, "This man was one of my crew. He tried to kill one of my other deck hands. Then he ran and I went after him and found him in the building at the back of the cannery. And that's where your boys found us."

George said, "I believe you. The problem is, now you know we're in the drug business. Besides that, because of this man," he paused as he pointed to John, "the son of our boss is dead. And our boss is very powerful and unforgiving. In fact he sent these two." He nodded at the two henchmen. First at the one by Barry's side, "that's Lee." Then at the other, "that one's Wong. There here to make sure we take care of our little problem, and that's you two."

John began to cry. "Please Mr. Franco, please let me go. I promise I won't say a thing."

Al started to laugh. But he stopped when George held up a hand and said, "You won't say a thing; about what? It doesn't matter boy. You gotta die. That's just the way it is."

Barry looked at George, "I suppose you're gonna kill me too?" George smiled, "Sorry."

George turned to Al, "Take em south past Addington. Dump them in deep water then sink their boat. Make it look like an accident. Tow our boat behind you, so you got a way home."

Al asked, "What about the crew?"

George frowned, "Didn't you hear me? I said get rid of them and I mean all of em."

Al persisted. "Well, what about Sissy?"

"Do whatever you want with her but kill her too."

Al smiled then signaled the two thugs, "Okay get these two on their feet and let's go."

As Barry was pulled to his feet he thought, "It's now or never." He stood up and then jammed his heel down along Lee's shin. The man cried out in pain and Barry pulled the gun from Lee's waist and turned to face the others. It was a desperate attempt at escape but in an instant he was knocked off his feet and to the floor. He lay there unconscious and bleeding from the gash on his head.

Holding the barrel of his automatic, George stood over Barry and asked, "Now can you three handle it from here? Or do I have to do everything myself?"

John sat paralyzed with fear.

George placed the gun back in his desk and left the room.

Al pointed to Barry and said, "Okay boys, pick this one up and let's get outa' here."

With Barry's limp body in tow, the five of them made their way down the steep stairway and out to the Harvester.

Sissy and Angie were in the galley with David when Al barged into the room with his gun drawn. Startled, Sissy asked, "What's going on?"

Before he could answer her, Lee entered the room and announced, "We took care of Geeser."

Al looked a little puzzled. "Whata ya mean?"

Lee answered, "Just following Mister Wang's orders. Geeser's dead."

With no show of emotion Al said, "Okay tie these three up and put em' with the other two. Let's get going now!"

They left Steamboat Bay with the five captives there on the back deck hidden from sight underneath a canvas tarp.

33

PURSUIT

The Harvester had a nine hour head start but engine problems and towing the unwieldy cruiser in the choppy sea had shortened its lead. Al kept the bow into the swells. He muttered, "I'll be glad when we sink this tub."

By ten o'clock Dylan caught sight of them off Security Cove on the southwest coast of Dall Island. He eased off on the throttle and the seine skiff slowed to a crawl. The Harvester was about a half mile away.

The two Chinese thugs having had little experience on the ocean were both sea sick and too nauseous to notice the little dot trailing them.

Al was busy either in the wheelhouse keeping the bow pointed into the swell or else down in the engine room tinkering with the engine. Finally, Al brought the Harvester to a stop. He walked aft to the back deck, smiled and said, "This is the place."

They pulled the tarp off their captives.

Al said, "If they find you, we don't want you tied up; wouldn't look natural." He smiled.

And then at gunpoint, one at a time, David, Barry, and Angie were untied and pushed overboard. After they untied Sissy, Al said to her, "I'll let you live if you're real nice to me." She thought for a moment then spit in his face and said, "Screw you," and jumped overboard.

Al wiped her spittle from his cheek, smiled as he looked after her and said, "woulda' been nice." Then he wrapped spare anchor chain around John Geeser's lifeless body and pitched it into the sea.

Al turned to Lee and Wong. "Okay boys, time to sink this boat and go home." Minutes later he opened a valve in the engine room and the Harvester began to flood. From the safety of their cabin cruiser they watched as Barry's boat slipped below the surface. Al moved the throttle forward and headed the cruiser back to Steamboat Bay.

Meantime still undetected, Dylan had circled around and come in from the west. He brought the skiff to where he had seen his friends enter the water but by that time the current had taken them a few hundred yards to the south. Fortunately, they remained calm and stayed together as best they could and managed to keep David's head above the water.

It was twilight and the visibility was declining. Compounding that was the wind and the blinding salt spray off the tops of the swells. Dylan kept on steering the skiff in larger and larger concentric rings, determined to find his friends. The water was cold and Dylan knew it was just a matter of time before hypothermia set in and then they would all drown.

Then as if by chance, or divine grace, he spotted Sissy's orange knit cap bobbing up and down about fifty yards off the port bow. Moments later Dylan was pulling them from the sea.

Barry managed to say, "Boy am I glad to see you." Dylan looked down at him and just said, "me too."

They were cold, pale, and shivering uncontrollably. They couldn't have lasted another fifteen minutes in that water. As they huddled together at the bottom of the skiff, Dylan covered them with a survival blanket and passed around his thermos of hot coffee and the smoked salmon strips, cheese, and cookies from the lunch box that Mary packed for him. He remembered her words, "This is for you just in case you get hungry."

Dylan put his arm around Sissy and gave her a warm kiss. He said, "Welcome back," and then, "I love you."

She looked at him and smiled, "Ditto."

About that time, Al picked up the field binoculars from the cruiser's dashboard and scanned the sea for witnesses (a habit from his fish poaching days). He spotted the seine skiff and announced, "Crap, looks like visitors."

Al called the cannery. "Yeah George, it's Al," pause, "Over."

"Yeah Al, what's up?" Pause, "Over."

"We got rid of the baggage," pause, "Over."

"Good, any problems?" Pause, "Over."

Al knew George wouldn't like what he was about to say. "Looks like someone in a seine skiff picked up some of our guests, I mean baggage," pause, "Over."

After a long tense pause the voice screamed, "Son of a bitch. Probably the kid off the Mary Ann who was here looking for the Harvester. If they make it back alive, we're dead! Understand? Make sure they don't." Pause, "Out."

The chase was on. It was a race through a choppy sea, south along the west coast of Dall Island. The skiffs two mile lead was rapidly shrinking as they headed for Cape Muzon. Barry looked back at the cruiser and said, "It'll be dark soon. If we can just make it around the cape and to the back side of Dall Island, we'll find a safe place to hide."

The skiffs lead had shrunk in half.

By this time, both Wong and Lee were sea sick and the color of chartreuse. Al had no pity whatsoever. He kept the throttle at three quarter speed and the cruiser powered over each swell. To say the least, theirs was a rough ride. It was a ten foot sea and the swells were running about eighteen feet apart; which meant that as their twenty foot boat cut across the top of each wave it would crash to the bottom of the following trough. The whole boat would shudder as green water came over the bow and the roof of the cabin.

Wong and Lee stayed in the cabin and held on for dear life. They took turns bent over vomiting into the toilet which made the stench inside the cabin terrible enough to finally force Wong outside and hang his head over the rail. Moments later they could hear his faint cry for help but from Al's perspective, Wong was no more than just dead weight and definitely not worth turning the cruiser around in that sea. He looked at Lee and said, "That's the way it goes. He shouldn't have gone outside."

And without so much as the slightest protest, Lee rose from his kneeling position, wiped the back of his hand across his lips, and sat back down onto the cabin's bench. He just sat there emotionless and stared out the window.

It was impossible to know what Lee was thinking, but then again, Al didn't care.

The wind picked up to gale force and the swells built to fifteen feet which forced both Al and Dylan to ease back on their throttles. Little by little, Al kept gaining on Dylan.

Dylan wiped the salt spray from his face and said, "They'll probably call the cannery and figure out that I came out here looking for you."

Barry nodded, "Most likely they've already done that."

Sissy smiled as they finally passed the cape's rocky shore. For her, this place was more than a spot on the chart. She turned to Dylan and said, "Don't worry. I know some really good hiding places where we'll be safe."

34

KAIGANI STRAIT

It was dark by the time the seine skiff rounded Cape Muzon and by that time the cannery's cruiser had closed to within a quarter mile. With an audible sigh of relief, Dylan turned the skiff north along the leeward side of Dall Island into calm water.

By the time the cruiser finally reached the cape the seine skiff was making its way up Kaigani Straight; a dangerous place of many unchartered rocks lying just below the surface; a place where boats foundered. But for Angie and Sissy this was a familiar place rich with Haida and Tlingit legends where as children they spent many happy days with their family camping and harvesting its rich resources.

By moonlight and an incoming tide they made their way into the safety of deeper water.

They passed by the abandoned village of Howkan where the Kaigani Haida had once lived and now was just ruin and rotting totems.

Sissy said, "Once a long time ago my great great grandfather and some of our people had been held prisoner in this place by the Haida."

Dylan asked, "so, what happened?"

She said, "They would all have been killed had it not been for a brave white man who came to their rescue. That was the time of the Tlingit-Haida wars. But that's another story."

Angie interrupted, "Sh!" Nobody spoke.

The cruisers searchlight appeared in the distance. Barry whispered, "They've slowed down to pick their way around the rocks."

The searchlight became smaller and smaller as the seine skiff's lead grew. Finally it disappeared from sight.

About midnight Sissy and Angie said almost in unison, "There Dylan, turn there." Try as he might, Dylan could not see what they were pointing at. It just looked like another dark cranny in the shoreline. But he obeyed and turned the skiff shoreward into a narrow channel.

The entrance was not much wider than the boat. After about a hundred feet or so, it opened into a small bay surrounded on all sides by dense forest.

All was calm and quiet except for an occasional calling wolf. The surface of the water was like a sheet of glass. And inland to the west, a mountain ridge illuminated by the setting moon rose three thousand feet above the forest.

Sissy said, "We call this place Hidden Cove."

They anchored the skiff in shallow water and waded to the shore. It felt good to sit on the beach.

Barry looked over at Dylan and said, "At first light though we've gotta leave here or they'll find us for sure and we'll be trapped. We've gotta beat the tide before it turns or we'll never make it through Tlevak Narrows." Then he said, "We're safe here for now."

No sooner had he said that than they could hear the unmistakable noise of an approaching diesel engine resonating through the darkness. Barry ordered everyone into the forest.

David was too weak to walk so Barry and Dylan hoisted him up by his armpits and the three scrambled off the beach for cover.

Barry turned to Dylan, "We'll jump them if they come ashore." All became dark as the moon set behind the mountain. They stayed hidden as a beam of light passed over their heads. They could hear the sound of the boat's aluminum hull slide onto the sandy beach. A few moments later, voices on the beach could be heard.

Barry whispered, "It's now or never."

So, like raving banshees waving driftwood clubs, they broke out of hiding and ran directly at the voices; and stopped.

35

THE TIDE TURNS

Caught in the beam of the flashlight, they were within ten feet of the source when a familiar voice called out, "Stop, it's me Ben!"

They came face-to-face with Ben and Too Tall. After a moment or two they realized that here indeed were their rescuers.

Then there were hugs and kisses and a flood of questions and answers.

They carried David to the beach and made him as comfortable as they could while Sissy dressed his wound with supplies from the Mary Ann's first aid kit. Then Ben opened a boxed lunch and passed it around.

Barry asked, "How'd you guys find us?"

Ben said, "It's a long story but here's what happened. Last night we pulled into Steamboat and you were gone. We found George Franco in the office and he told us Barry went back to Sitka and that he never even saw Dylan. We knew that was a lie, especially since we found the Harvester's seine skiff," he pointed to the skiff on the beach, "hidden behind the cannery dock."

Barry interjected, "They cut it loose from our stern."

Ben continued, "Anyway, we convinced Franco to tell us which way you guys really went. It took some convincing," he rubbed his swollen knuckles, "but he decided to tell the truth. Also a guy off a sail boat tied to the cannery's float said he saw a seiner down by the south end of Dall Island. There was no reason for a seiner to be there so we guessed it was probably you."

Dylan asked, "but how did you know to look here?" Ben grinned at Sissy and Angie. "That was easy. The three of us used to play here when we were kids. Hidden Cove was our secret hiding place and chances were, you'd be here."

Too Tall said, "We've got a surprise for you."

He made a quick trip to the skiff and returned with cardboard box which he set at Angie's feet.

She opened it and exclaimed thankfully, "Dry clothes, you guys brought dry clothes!"

Too Tall said, "Yep, we figured you'd need em."

No sooner said and the girls disappeared into the forest with their dry wardrobe. Ben continued, "So anyway Marvin and Double Shot stayed at Steamboat, keeping Franco and a couple of his crew company while they waited for the state troopers to show up. Too Tall and me cut across the north end of Dall and here we are."

Ben asked, "what about all of you?"

Barry told them what happened and finished by saying, "Al and his two hoods are out there now cruising the beaches looking for us. We've seen their search light."

Angie and Sissy kept watch over David. He had lost a lot of blood and his wound was badly infected. Sissy told Dylan, "He has a bad fever. I'm not sure whether he can make it much longer. We've got to get him home."

Dylan said, "We will."

They sat there under the clear starlit summer sky and passed around Too Tall's bottle of bourbon. Even though they couldn't risk a campfire, they were warm. Sissy sat close to Dylan.

At sunrise, Dylan motored the seine skiff north, out of the cove. Ben sat hidden from view on the bottom of the boat. He held his deer rifle at the ready.

It was a brisk tranquil morning with patches of fog scattered across the water's calm surface.

The high pitched calls of Bald Eagles, awakened in their roosts, echoed from the tops of the giant cedars while the drama unfolded below.

As if on cue, the cruiser appeared from around an outcrop of the rocky shore about a half mile to the south.

The trap was about to be set and Al Franco was the unsuspecting quarry.

Al smiled at Lee and said, "We're gaining on em. As soon as we get along side, we'll start shooting. I've had enough of this shit. I want them dead."

Al focused on the seine skiff. Dylan's lead was getting shorter and shorter. Al mumbled to himself, "Now I've got ya. Ya bastard."

So intent on his prize, he never noticed the second skiff behind him. To Al's surprise, Dylan brought the skiff to a stop and at the right moment, Ben sat up firing his rifle.

The first round caught Lee in the chest. He fell overboard like an oversized halibut carcass, dead.

Al looked back at the floating corpse and then back at the speeding skiff with Barry and Too Tall armed and firing.

This was a tight situation and Al knew immediately what was happening. He had long history of crossed paths with the Coast Guard and state troopers. As a juvenile delinquent both he and his brother had "rap sheets" a mile long for a variety of petty crimes. Eventually they were both convicted on narcotics charges and spent time in federal prison.

He always evaded capture before by acts of sheer daring and recklessness, stupidity, and luck. This time was no different. And so at full speed he turned the cruiser back toward Barry. Just before they collided he turned his wheel hard to starboard. The cruiser spun around and generated a wave which rolled the skiff almost to the point of capsizing. Barry was just able to hang on but Too Tall was thrown to the starboard rail. Under a hail of bullets, the cruiser turned north and sped past Dylan.

So with Dylan and Barry in hot pursuit, Al ran for the little bay at the end of Tlevak Strait where for the moment, the water was glass calm. And Tlevak Narrows was his only way out.

36

A WALL OF WATER

Maybe it was Karma catching up with Al. Whatever it was, the previous night's high tide was twelve feet above the average normal. When the morning tide shifted to extreme low, the shallow bay drained quickly. So quickly in fact, that the water level beyond the north end of Tlevak Narrows was ten feet higher than the bay's surface; and near the center of the bay was its notorious whirlpool.

Like a speeding freight train the wall of water moved through the pass into the shallow bay. Anything in its way was destroyed; Al Franco and the cruiser were in the way.

Dylan, Ben, Barry and Too Tall kept at a safe distance and waited long enough to see Al disappear beneath the wave. Then the two skiffs headed back to Hidden Cove. By the time they returned with Sissy, Angie, and David the water levels on both sides of the narrows had equalized, the whirlpool was gone, and passage from the bay was again safe.

For a while they searched for Al. They found bits and mangled pieces of the cruiser that were scattered along the shoreline but no Al. So they continued on through the narrows.

On the other side of the pass, a thick fog lifted to reveal a sunlit and cloudless turquoise blue sky. They would be home soon.

It was a fine day to be alive.

EPILOGUE

When they arrived at Klawock they were greeted at the dock by family and friends. David James was flown to the hospital in Ketchikan and soon recovered from his injuries.

George Franco stood trial for drug trafficking and murder. He pleaded "not guilty" and testified that it was his brother Al and the two thugs who killed John Geeser. And furthermore, that he had no involvement in any wrongdoing whatsoever.

Lee Wang's partially decomposed body had been discovered by the state troopers. It was an open and shut case against George but the trial ended with a deadlocked jury and the case against him was dismissed.

Later after the trial, the FBI investigators were tipped off that two of the jury members had been bribed by Chin Wang.

It seems however, that after George was released he was tracked down by the Chinese Mafia and escorted to Hong Kong where he was brought before the unforgiving Chin Wang. George was never seen again.

Steamboat Bay cannery was seized and placed on the auction block by the Federal Government as an asset of Hong Kong Ltd. Export/Import. Its role in international drug trafficking was discovered during the course of the trial.

After the loss of the Harvester, Barry quit fishing temporarily and used the money from the insurance policy to purchase Steamboat Bay Cannery plus its adjacent properties. Barry (with the help of Dylan) renovated the old cannery and turned it into a trophy fishing lodge and fish buying station.

Barry and Angie are still engaged. After two more seasons, Marvin finally retired and turned the Mary Ann over to Ben who married a local girl. They have two beautiful girls that are growing like weeds. Marvin and Mary are proud grandparents who intentionally spoil the girls.

Dylan and Sissy also married. Soon afterward, auntie Dorothy took them for a boat ride on Klawock Lake. They beached their boat on an isolated shore. It was beautiful place nestled among the cedars.

Dorothy explained that it was the family homestead and she gave it to them as a wedding present. The collapsed remains of an old log cabin stood next to a deep clear creek. She took their hands and said, "This was my great grandmother's house. She had been captured by the Haida but was rescued by a white man who later became her husband. That was many years ago when the Tlingit and Haida were at war."

Not far from what used to be the cabin's entrance stood an old broken totem pole. Weather and time conspired to destroy most of its carved figures but halfway up the old pole was a patch of moss that caught Dylan's eye. He brushed it away to expose a pair of crossed harpoons.

The season was fall and dog salmon crowded the creek.